FRANKIE TAKES A BOW

COOPERATIVE REALM

NICKY PENTTILA

ISBN 978-1-943192-42-7

The story, all names, characters, and incidents portrayed are fictitious. No identification with actual persons (living or deceased), places, buildings, and products is intended or should be inferred.

Book Cover by John A. Spillane

I

FRANKIE TAKES A BOW

CHAPTER
ONE

THE SPEAR'S kitchen smelled like burnt toast and victory.

Frankie leaned against the L-shaped galley counter, inhaling the familiar cocktail of industrial soap and cyvlossic kibble, overlaid by the scent of her failed attempt at an "authentic Wala-style breakfast." The dark rye toast had turned to charcoal while she'd been trying to figure out how to fold the spinach and dried fish into the creamy rice. But even the acrid smell couldn't dampen her mood.

They were home. Her ship, her rules.

Her slightly scorched breakfast.

Spike sprawled across the back of their favorite dining nook, the one closest to the door, past the round center table in the center of the kitchen. Her scruffy gray-black-orange fur spread in every direction like she'd been hit by an electrostatic burst. One massive paw dangled, occasionally batting at a suspicious-looking tear in the orange padding on the bench back of the U-shaped nook with the kind of lazy disdain only a cyvlossic could manage.

New kibble must've been good.

Frankie grabbed the "Galaxy's Best Captain" mug Beth had given her and poured real coffee—not the synthetic swill that tasted like burnt rubber, but actual beans from the agricultural station near Smithson Station. The smell alone was worth the price. Rich, dark, with hints of chocolate and home and not being sneaky for once.

She settled into her usual spot in the breakfast nook, across the table from Spike, sinking into the battered orange cushions that had molded themselves to her shape over hundreds of meals. The gray metal table still had that sticky spot near the edge where she'd spilled honey last week. Or was it two weeks ago? Time blurred together in the black between jump points.

The seedling Tala from White Moon Landing had given her caught the morning-tinted light from the overhead panels, its red-tipped tendrils already creeping up the wall beside the reheater. In just a week (or two), it had claimed a quarter meter of vertical space, creating a delicate lattice of green against the dull gray bulkhead. Every time Frankie looked at it, she remembered White Moon, quantum dots, and the fact that Spike had a data port hidden somewhere in that matted-fur belly.

And she could use it.

On the black speckled rubber-metal floor, beside the PermaPot holding the seedling, two half-empty paint cans waited like patient promises. Blue Sky and Butter Morning. She'd been staring at them for days, and then staring at the utilitarian gray walls in the kitchen. In the hallways. In her bedroom.

But something held her back. Indecisiveness? Not really. Imposter syndrome, more like.

She'd bought this ship, and the cargo routes it was licensed for, from Old Peters more than a year ago. Since then, it had been shot at, stunk up for a month by a shipment of glimmerantin beans, and used for rescuing damsels in distress (well, cyvlossics who wanted to run away from home).

So why did she still feel like a visitor? Like the Spear wasn't really hers—not deep down. It was still Old Peters' ship in all the ways that mattered. She was just borrowing it.

Go on. Make it yours.

Easier said than done.

Her wrist comm beeped a reminder, and Beth's message hovered in the air again, purple-gold priority seal mocking her procrastination.

Call me. No, it's good news.

Three days. Three days she'd been finding excuses. The nav array needed recalibrating (it didn't). The number two escape pod was making a funny noise (barely audible). The cargo manifest for their next run required extensive review (it was two lines long).

Frankie pressed "remind me later," again, and the message disappeared.

Good news from Beth usually meant someone in the Cooperative Realm's central government had actually done their job. Another orphan support program had squeezed through committee, maybe. Or Beth had been promoted again and wanted Frankie to attend the ceremony. Which meant formalwear. Which meant a trip to Zichi. To the Capital, with its empty air and perfect manners and memories sharp enough to cut.

She loved her friend, the only one she'd really kept after the destruction of her home planet. And Beth was a great cook—probably could make a Wala-style breakfast in her sleep. But Beth loved the Capital, and the politics, and the whole song and dance.

And why shouldn't she? She was good at it. Not like Frankie, poster child for the Child Orphans of Wala. If only that photo, the one that caught everyone's imagination—and their sick, sad pity —had been of Beth instead of her.

The comm beeped again. New message: *Frankie, seriously. Call me.*

Then: *I can see you're receiving these.*

Then: *I'm using the priority channel in five minutes.*

"Shit." Frankie sat straight. She looked at Spike. "Beth's on the rampage."

Spike yawned, displaying an impressive array of teeth that had made more than one dock worker reconsider their life choices. Somehow, the gesture conveyed both *I told you so* and *this is what you get for procrastinating.*

The priority channel meant encryption so thick it made the air taste metallic. It meant real-time video that would show every stain on her tank top, every wild curl escaping her hasty ponytail.

"Maybe I should change?" She looked down at herself. The lubricant stain from fixing the gray-water recycler had dried into an interesting pattern that looked almost artistic if you squinted. At least the tank top was purple. Used to be purple, it actually looked more lilac now.

Spike's tail twitched. One. Precise. Flick.

Frankie slouched back into the bench seat, and took another sip of the wonderful coffee.

The comm screen erupted, a circle of purple and gold, the Regent's seal filling the small table between Frankie and Spike with officious light. Priority override. No more hiding.

Frankie's finger hovered over the accept button. In the background, that panel in the wall buzzed—a loose connection she'd been meaning to fix since buying the ship. The coffee maker gurgled. The seedling rustled in the circulation vent's breeze. All the sounds of home, about to be invaded by—

She hit accept.

Beth's face materialized above the table.

Oh, no. Oh, no no no.

Her best friend was glowing. Not the metaphorical glow of happiness, though that too, but actually luminous. Like someone had replaced her blood with liquid starlight. Her ebony hair, which Frankie remembered in practical braids or a graceful swoop, was now an architectural marvel of loops and spirals that defied at least three laws of physics. Her formal jacket was cerulean blue when it wasn't shifting between colors

And her smile. Frankie had seen that exact smile once before, when they were twelve and Beth had figured out how to hack the Complex's dessert dispensers. They'd eaten chocolate until they were sick, laughing on the bathroom floor at three in the morning, sugar-drunk and invincible.

"Finally!" Beth said, and even her voice sparkled. "I was about to send a diplomatic courier. Do you know how much paperwork that involves?"

"You wouldn't."

"I absolutely would. I've already filled out the first three forms." Beth leaned forward, and the projection flickered slightly —even priority channels had their limits out here in the edge systems. "Listen. I have news! Amazing news. Life-changing, universe-altering, practice-your-surprised-face news."

Frankie's stomach began a slow slide toward her grav boots. In her experience, life-changing news was rarely the good kind.

"Beth—"

"I'm getting married!"

The words hung in the recycled air like unexploded ordnance. Spike's other eye opened. Both ears swiveled forward. Even the buzzing panel seemed to pause.

"Married," Frankie repeated, testing the word. It felt foreign in her mouth, like speaking High Galactic after months of dock-worker slang. "You. Getting married. To another person. On purpose."

"I know!" Beth clasped her hands together, and Frankie noticed the ring—subtle by Capital standards, which meant it probably cost more than the Spear. "I can barely believe it myself. But Frankie, he's wonderful. He's brilliant and kind and he actually listens when I talk about agricultural subsidies. He has this project with singing orchids—they harmonize based on light frequencies—and yesterday he spent three hours explaining the bio-acoustic principles and I understood maybe half of it but I wasn't bored once!"

The words tumbled out in a rush so unlike Beth's usual measured diplomatic cadence. This was twelve-year-old Beth, pre-politics Beth, Beth who used to practice speeches in their shared bathroom while Frankie threw soap bubbles at her for emphasis.

"That's..." Frankie groped for words. "That's wonderful. Who's the lucky—"

"Alain diCimino." Beth's glow dimmed slightly, watching Frankie's face.

The Regent's second son.

The kitchen tilted. Or maybe that was just Frankie's inner ear giving up. She gripped the table's edge, fingers finding the sticky spot like an anchor.

"The Regent's..." The words wouldn't come.

"I know what you're thinking." Beth's expression shifted, political training reasserting itself. "It's calculated. It's climbing. I'm selling out even more than I already have. But it's not like that. He doesn't even want the succession. His older brother can have all that nonsense. Alain just wants to grow his singing plants and maybe teach at the university someday. He makes me laugh, Frankie. When was the last time someone at the Complex made me actually laugh?"

Frankie couldn't answer that. She was still processing "Regent's son." The Regent, who'd taken them in after Wala imploded. Who'd dressed them up like dolls and paraded them through the systems as symbols of Cooperative benevolence. Who'd meant well, probably, but who'd never understood that kindness could be its own kind of cage.

"Wedding's in six weeks," Beth burbled, oblivious. "On Zichi, of course. The whole Complex is already in preparation mode. You should see the flower arguments. Someone suggested Orr roses and three senators nearly declared war. The Trade Committee actually issued a formal statement about 'inappropriate outer-moon-centric displays.' It's ridiculous and I love every minute of it."

"Six weeks?" Frankie's voice came out strangled. Spike poured herself onto the bench and padded around to Frankie. The cyvlossic flopped down beside her, her head on Frankie's thigh. Without thinking, Frankie set her hand on Spike's flank, and grasped a clump of warm fur.

"That's... soon," she finally said.

"I know! But we didn't want to wait, and besides..." Beth's expression shifted again, becoming softer and somehow more intense. "I chose the date specially. To make that horrible anniversary into something beautiful."

The tilting sensation became a full spin. Frankie knew what was coming. Knew it in her bones, in the place where trauma lived.

"The twenty-second." Beth's voice was gentle now, careful. "The Wala anniversary. I thought... I thought we could transform it. Make it a day about love and new beginnings instead of..."

Instead of endings. Instead of fire and ash and a nine-year-old girl in a famous photo, staring at the camera like the world had broken.

Which it had.

"Oh." Beth must have seen something in Frankie's face. "Oh, honey, I didn't think—I mean, I did think, I thought it would be healing—"

"It's fine," Frankie said automatically. Her hands were shaking. Spike started to purr. Two decades—more—since Wala was destroyed. Two decades since she became an orphan, a ward, a symbol, a footnote in history books.

And Beth wanted to paste a wedding over it like fixing a hull breach with decorative tape.

"It's not fine." Beth leaned forward, close enough that Frankie could see the worry lines that politics had etched around her eyes. "I can see that. But Frankie, that's exactly why I need you there. You're my best friend. You're the only one who understands what that day means. The others…"

"The others?"

Beth's expression went carefully neutral, diplomat-blank. "I reached out to all of them. Every surviving orphan. They… declined. Very politely. But firmly."

Of course they did. Frankie could imagine those conversations. So sorry, Beth. Previous engagement. Can't possibly make it. Send our best. Please don't ever call us again.

"But you'll come." It wasn't quite a question. "You have to come. It won't be right without you."

Frankie closed her eyes. What had they said to each other? "My door is open. My hand is yours." Anything, for Beth.

Anything but this.

"It's just, I… this is a lot."

"I know," Beth looked off screen. Was someone there? "I know it is. And I know you hate the Capital, and formal events make you break out in stress hives, and the last time you wore a dress we were—what, twelve?"

"Fourteen. That diplomatic reception where I spilled sauce on the Praxian ambassador."

"Right! See? Memories." Beth's smile was wobbly now, real emotion breaking through the polish. "Good memories mixed with the awful ones, but still. We survived, Frankie. We made it out. And now I'm getting married to a man who makes plants sing, and I want my best friend there to tell me if I'm being an idiot."

Frankie looked at her cup, the coffee growing cold. At Spike, in full noisy sprawl. At Beth, whose shoulders were stiff with worry.

"Don't answer right now." Beth straightened, pulling her political face back on like armor. "Think about it. But think fast. I need to know soon for security clearances and seating charts and about a thousand other ridiculous details that apparently require Senate subcommittee approval."

"Security clearances. Right." Because attending a wedding on Zichi meant background checks and diplomatic protocols and media cameras and people asking about that day, that picture, that moment when she learned that the universe had teeth.

"I love you," Beth said suddenly. "Whatever you decide. I love you and I miss you and I wish… I wish things were different."

"Yeah," Frankie said. "Me too."

The call ended, leaving purple-gold afterimages floating in the air. Frankie lifted her hands to her wayward hair, closed her eyes, and tried to imagine herself at a society wedding in the heart of everything she'd run from.

"Well," she said to Spike. "Shit."

Spike yawned. The purring continued.

The Spear hummed around them, steady and sure. Somewhere in the walls, that panel resumed its buzzing. The seedling rustled in the air from the vents. The freezer sighed.

Home. Her home. Her burnt-toast-scented, snowman-shaped, jump-gate traveling home.

Six weeks until she'd have to leave it.

CHAPTER
TWO

FRANKIE HAD BEEN STARING at the blank message screen for forty-seven minutes.

Dear Beth, I'm so happy for you but I can't possibly—

Delete.

Beth! Congratulations! Unfortunately, I have a prior—

Delete.

Beth, I would rather eat liver-flavored protein paste for a year than attend a formal Cooperative Realm wedding on the anniversary of our planet's destruction.

Definitely delete.

She slouched deeper into the wide, comfy pilot's chair, feet propped on the nav console in direct violation of every safety protocol she'd ever learned. The Spear's bridge wrapped around her like a gray metal cocoon, all curved surfaces and blinking lights and nothing that needed her attention since the autopilot was on. The pilot's seat—worn in all the right places—welcomed her in ways the vast cargo hold or even her own quarters could never quite manage.

A pilot, she belonged here. A captain? Yeah, right.

Through the main viewport, the stars wheeled slowly past. They were in a lazy orbit around Smithson Station, waiting for their next cargo assignment and definitely not hiding from ceremonial obligations. She had the inset lights on half, that perfect twilight glow that made the five-monitor array pop against the mainly matte gray composite of the console. The two wide screens on the bottom, three above, had guided her through asteroid fields and ion storms alike. The gentle electronic hum of the ship's systems created a lullaby she could feel in her chest as much as hear with her ears.

The air tasted different here than in the rest of the Spear—metallic with a hint of ozone from the electronics, but also carrying the faint musk of Spike's fur—everywhere!—and a persistent note of coffees past. The environmental systems could scrub anything from the air, but some scents just became part of the ship's signature, like the ghost of Old Peters' pipe smoke that sometimes seemed to materialize in the corners.

A shuffle, and a sniff, signaled Spike was coming on deck. Frankie didn't need to turn to know it was the cyvlossic—the subtle change in the room's atmosphere, the shift in scents from somewhat sterile to something earthier, wilder, was unmistakable. And the fact that no one else was on board.

The open door from the hallway was deliberately wide. Old Peters had insisted every passageway, entrance, and tool on the Spear accommodate beings of various sizes and abilities. Spike took full advantage of it, pressing the door panel controls near the floor to get into rooms, banging her shoulder into cupboard doors that would open with a gentle push. And here, claiming the co-pilot's seat with a single sinuous motion. The chair, built to accommodate a generously-proportioned human (and Old Peters when he had to wear the back brace), seemed almost inadequate for the cyvlossic. But she made it work.

The blue glow from the console screens cast strange shadows

through her uneven coat, making her look even more other-worldly than usual. One pointed ear, tipped with a distinctive black tuft, tracked Frankie's movements while the rest of her appeared to settle down to sleep.

As if. Spike's sharp, mostly green eyes might be closed, but Frankie knew the cyvlossic missed nothing. Those eyes, when open, held an unsettling intelligence that reminded anyone who took the time to look that Spike was no ordinary grossly over-sized cat. Konrad Orr's synthetic "enhancements" had created something far beyond ordinary, though Spike herself stayed mum on the details of her origins or capabilities.

"Maybe I could contract a communicable disease," Frankie mused aloud.

Spike's ear twitched. Dismissive.

"You're right. Beth would just send one of the Regent's doctors or something." Frankie deleted her latest attempt and started over. How did you tell your best friend that her happiness was giving you hives?

The comm panel chirped. Not Beth's priority channel, thank the void, but the other highly encrypted connection. Systems Analysis.

Spike's ear twitched. She lifted her head to look at the console.

Maybe Bruce had another job for them. One that would take them even farther out into edge space. And would take months. And had to be started right away.

"Accept connection," Frankie called out to Ship so she wouldn't have to sit up. The ship's intelligence connected the call.

The central monitor flickered, and Bruce's face filled the screen. His dark square visage was made even more angular by the strong side light in his fake-wood-paneled office. His thick black hair ended with geometric precision at the same level as his equally dense sideburns, connected by a sharply trimmed mustache that looked like it had been drawn with a ruler. Everything about the man screamed precision and control, from his perfectly pressed collar to the way his eyes catalogued every detail they landed on.

Bruce was the kind of person who could blend perfectly into any bureaucratic setting while simultaneously monitoring six covert operations across three star systems. As a manager at Systems Analysis—or SystA, as insiders called it—he coordinated field operatives from the organization's headquarters on Rosing Station, strategically positioned at the crossroads of major trade routes but conveniently out of the common way.

SystA's official purpose was to gather, analyze, and disseminate critical information across Cooperative Space—a data-processing company that maintained stability and security by identifying threats before they materialized. Unofficially, it rescued lost people, ensured bad actors had worse luck, and generally tried to make this slice of the galaxy a better place.

"Frankie! he boomed. "Spike! How's my favorite stealth team?" He frowned in Spike's direction. "Molting?"

Spike lurched up to sitting. When she sat on her haunches, Spike's head came even with Frankie's. She glowered at Bruce.

"Chatty as ever, I see. Well, good work at White Moon Landing. Your report was… concise."

Frankie shrugged. "You said to keep it short."

"I said to include relevant details. You failed to describe the quantum processor."

"Figured Spike would do that, being the tech genius and all." Frankie glanced at her partner, who was now staring at Bruce with the kind of intensity usually reserved for prey. "How did you—never mind."

Bruce knew everything. It was his most annoying quality. But he also loved fairytales, didn't argue about their expense reports, and knew where to get the best food on every moon, base or planet.

"Your next assignment—"

"Outer edge space?" Frankie interrupted. "Leaving now? We're ready."

"Ah, no." Bruce ran a hand down his immaculate beard. "Interesting times for the Great Houses on Zichi."

Frankie's mouth snapped shut. Spike's ears swiveled forward.

Zichi.

"We're nowhere near Zichi," Frankie said, hearing the whine in her voice, ignoring the glare that Spike was giving her. "There must be another team closer."

Bruce rattled on as if he hadn't heard her.

"Orr intel has gone sloppy. We can't tell if Konrad is sick, or if someone else is at the wheel. Our monitors on their cyvlossic network have degraded—we see that packets are still being sent, but the response channel's gone dark." His expression didn't change, but something in his tone made the hair on Frankie's neck stand up. "The kind of changes that usually precede significant political realignment. Find out who's actually holding the leash now."

Great.

Beth was probably in the middle of it.

Just great.

"And you want us to—"

"Nothing official. But since you'll be on Zichi anyway—"

"I'm not going to Zichi."

"—for the Blais-diCimino wedding—"

"I'm not going to the wedding."

"—you could keep your ears open. Observe. Report anything unusual." Bruce's eyebrow rose. "Unofficially."

"Bruce." Frankie sat up straighter, feet hitting the deck with a clang. "I'm not going to Zichi. I'm not going to the wedding. I'm staying right here in my ship, doing absolutely nothing except my standard shipping routes and possibly painting my bedroom."

"I see." Bruce's tone suggested he saw entirely too much. "Fridrika Styles Faldasdotter." He said it correctly, "steel-ays," like people on Wala used to say it. Like nobody said it now.

Devious. Kind, but devious.

"If you change your mind, the situation with the Great Houses is… delicate." He tapped his lower lip twice. "The kind of delicate that could affect trade routes, supply chains, the price of coffee on twelve different stations."

"You're trying to manipulate me with coffee?"

"Is it working?"

"No." Maybe, a little. The good coffee came through Zichi-controlled routes. "Besides, I don't have clearance for Capital society anymore. They'd spot me as edge-space trash in five seconds."

"Your diplomatic status was never revoked."

Frankie stared at him. "Impossible. I left. I very specifically and dramatically left."

"The Regent has a long memory and a longer reach. Your codes are still active. Your clearances are still valid. Your place at the table, so to speak, is still set." Bruce's expression softened. "They never let you go, Frankie. They just let you think they did."

The bridge suddenly felt too small. Fifteen years of running, and she'd been on a very long leash the whole time.

"I have to go," Frankie said. "Ship things. Urgent ship things."

"Of course. But Frankie? If you do happen to find yourself on Zichi, unofficially observing unusual patterns among the Great Houses, I would be very interested in your unofficial observations."

"I'm not—"

The connection cut. Bruce always had the last word.

Frankie slumped back in her chair, staring at the stars. They stared back, unhelpfully silent.

"No," she said to Spike. "Whatever you're thinking, no."

Spike stretched, a process that involved all four legs extending in different directions and her spine achieving configurations that would make a yoga master weep. She then sat up, fixed Frankie with both green eyes, and said in her steel-sawing voice:

"Zichi."

"No."

"My vacation. My choice." Each word came out like gravel in a cement mixer, the result of whatever had damaged her vocal cords long ago. "You promised."

She had, indeed, promised. The last two vacations had gone south, relaxation-wise. That one deep under water had even made Spike sick.

"I promised you could pick our next vacation destination. I didn't say when."

"Now." Spike's eyes gleamed. "Pet spas. Mineral baths. Heated stones."

"You hate being groomed."

Spike's tail swished, unmoved. "Sun. Real tuna."

"Spike—"

The cyvlossic closed her eyes a moment, maybe sending a message. Or, actually, powering up the other big monitor. An advertisement for Paws of Paradise started to play. At least the audio was off.

"Holistic wellness?" But Frankie leaned closer. The pet spa actually listed cyvlossics as potential clients. One shot showed a sleek, pampered cyvlossic, all cream and honey, lounging on silk cushions while attendants brushed its perfect fur. "How many cyvlossics are even on Zichi?"

Spike was one of an endangered species, supposedly. From an out-system planet, supposedly. Konrad Orr had obtained permission—who knew how—to try to breed them, in an effort to stabilize the population. What he'd really done was make a litter of enhanced hybrids, with implanted memory boosters, stronger skeletons, voice boxes, who knew what.

"All of them," Spike said.

Of course. Frankie sat back. Orr's cyvlossics were spies. "Gifts" to each of the Great Houses, which had no idea of their special skills. The Great families merely knew they were rare, and valuable. As status. Of course, they'd bring them to the capital city.

Spike's expression was pure innocence, which on her face looked like she was planning murder. "Excellent vacation. Besides. You need to see Beth."

"I don't—"

"And Morgan."

Frankie's protest died in her throat. Morgan. The only person besides Beth who might make Zichi bearable. The charming disaster of an Orr who'd somehow become... what? Friend was too simple. Complicated was too vague.

She thought of his ridiculous color-changing clothes and his terrible timing and his too-floppy hair and the way he'd looked at her when—

No. Bad train of thought. At least he'd found Celine, and stopped looking that way at Frankie. She hoped.

"I am not calling Morgan Orr. What would I say? 'Hey, Morgan, want to be my plus-one to the most politically charged wedding of the decade? We're making new memories to cover up that atrocity your father caused."

"Don't call. Surprise him."

"That's worse!"

"Romantic."

"It's not—we're not—" Frankie gestured helplessly. "It's complicated."

Spike padded over to the nav console and pulled up a star chart with one paw. A direct route to Zichi. Five weeks travel.

Shit.

Spike pushed the engine specs. Now the estimate was four weeks.

"We're not pushing my engines for a pet spa."

"For Beth."

"That's cheating."

Spike highlighted a spot on the route. Minerva Station. "Great noodles."

She did like their noodles. Dammit.

Well, they could head that way, and if she changed her mind, Frankie and Spear could pull away. Stay at Minerva station. Fly to some new moon.

"Fine." Frankie threw herself into the back of the chair and put her feet up on the console again. "I'll write Beth tomorrow."

Spike sat back from the console. She licked a front paw.

A minute later, a ping on Frankie's wristcom. Beth.

Fantastic! Can't wait to see you! Who's Spike?

"What. Did. You. Do?"

Spike didn't even have the grace to look guilty.

Frankie was never going to partner with a hacker again. Never, ever.

But she had to admit, the cyvlossic was right. Frankie was also never going to say no to Beth, not in the end. Whatever terribleness lay ahead, seeing Beth glow was worth it.

One of them should glow.

Four weeks to Zichi. Four weeks to remember how to be Citizen Styles again.

She was definitely going to need better clothes.

CHAPTER
THREE

THE SPEAR DROPPED out of transit space with its usual shudder-thunk, and there it was. Zichi.

Home.

Not-home.

The word stuck in Frankie's throat like recycled protein paste.

She'd forgotten how blue it was. Not the cerulean and sapphire of planets with lots of oceans, but the deepest blue that came from one giant sea. From this distance, the single massive continent looked like someone had pressed a dusty thumb into the center of deep velvet, leaving a brown-red bruise surrounded by a thin ring of green. The fertile coastal strip where everyone lived, pressed between desert and sea.

The planet's small-moon-sized orbital station grew larger in her viewport. It had expanded since she'd left. Two new rings spun out from the original cylindrical structure like growth rings on a tree. More traffic, too. The geometric precision of the shipping lanes made her inwardly sigh with familiarity. Everything moving in perfect synchronized patterns, every ship in its designated slot, every trajectory optimized for efficiency.

So Cooperative it hurt.

The Spear sidled into the approach pattern among all the other incoming traffic, and Frankie let the autopilot take over. Her ship looked exactly like what it was against the sleek Cooperative vessels—a joke. No, a working trader's vessel that just happened to be shaped like a snowman, three stacked spheres, not a bit of it sleek. Carbon scoring on the hull that she hadn't bothered to buff out. A mismatched panel on the starboard side from that incident near Cantas Station. Real ship, real wear, real life.

Frankie wasn't paying the docking fees—artificially increased for the wedding, she'd just bet. Ship was taking them to a transient dock, and then would pilot itself out to one of the parking lots far outside the travel lanes.

No quick getaway.

As she powered down the pilot's console, she caught her reflection in a darkened monitor screen and almost didn't recognize herself. Her short, dark hair—slashed at an angle from just above her left ear down to her right jaw in the back, the bangs making a similar slash in the front—was growing out a bit at the edges, but at least it was her natural color now, no more disguises. The severe cut would have sent her deportment instructors into fits, but there was no time to grow it out now. She wore her plainest trader clothes: practical gray-green tunic, black cargo pants with actual pockets. Nothing that screamed money or connections. Nothing that would make anyone look twice.

Perfect. The less attention, the better.

Spike flowed off her perch on the co-pilot's chair with liquid grace. They'd be leaving by the "captain's door," through a tiny hall and double airlock just outside the pilot's room. Frankie tapped the control pad on her travel trunk—a refurbished small Skoll Shipping container, painted green but fooling no one—to make it float.

Spike was already halfway down the tiny hall. Frankie took one last look around her ship—her space, her rules, her life—then squared her shoulders and followed.

The mural-sized star-system map above the dozen kiosks at the security checkpoint had sprouted new gold highlights since her last visit—fresh planets, moons, stations. Welcome to the Cooperative Realm.

More like the Acquisitive Realm.

The security checkpoint had been upgraded. Again. The bank of biometric scanners hummed at a frequency that made Frankie's back teeth ache, reading who knew what—DNA, electromagnetic signature, probably her last three meals and her grandmother's maiden name. Her hand was already reaching for the correct bioscan pad before she consciously remembered its location. Muscle memory, apparently, survived longer than trauma responses. Interesting.

"Documentation." The security officer looked bored until she glanced at Spike, then her expression shifted to mild alarm. "Is that—"

"Companion Animal Class 3," Frankie said smoothly, holding out the pad, using her free hand to brush back the short, angled strands of hair from her face. "All permits in order."

Spike chose that moment to yawn, displaying her impressive dental array.

"I… see." The officer scanned the documents, then frowned at her screen. "Stand by."

Frankie's chest tightened. Had her codes expired? Been flagged? She kept her expression neutral while internally calculating how fast she could get back to the Spear. It wouldn't be released from dock until they had cleared decontamination and security.

"Oh. Orphan access. How inspiring," The officer looked up at her, a bit too long, the way tourists admired museum relics.

Frankie felt the old label clamp around her throat like a child-proof collar.

The officer processed them through quickly after that. Frankie collected their documents and tried not to notice how her hand wanted to tuck the skinny tablet into her tunic at the precise angle she'd been taught—documents at heart level, always accessible, never visible.

Spike stuck close to Frankie's side, companion animal-like, while her green box trailed in their wake. They walked up the long ramp to the exit.

They were halfway there when it hit her. The first whisper of station air, that collision of cloying perfumes, fish bread, and despair. Frankie's whole body went rigid. She stopped walking, forcing a couple people behind her to veer off, muttering.

It smelled like childhood. Like formal dinners she'd rather forget. Like standing very still while someone adjusted her formal robes and told her to remember who she represented.

Spike had not stopped. She turned around and ran back to bang against Frankie's legs. The familiar weight and warmth anchored her to the present. To who she was now. She started to move again.

They emerged into the main thoroughfare of Ring C, and Frankie hit overwhelm immediately. This time, she stepped to the side, to the fake stucco wall, to let the others pass.

Everywhere in the bright open space, noisy people in this season's CapCity fashion. Apparently shoulder augments were in, creating sharp silhouettes that made everyone look like angry triangles with legs. Hemlines had dropped to mid-calf but were slit to the hip in geometric patterns. Colors ran to deep purples and electric blues, with metallic threads that caught the station's bright overhead lights. Big hair, as usual, but the color palettes had changed.

And the makeup. The traditional maroon lips had gone

deeper, almost black-red, while the kohl had evolved into elaborate patterns—geometric again, no more swirls—that extended past the eyes. Cheek gems glinted like tears or stars, depending on how the light hit them.

Frankie, in her plain trader clothes with her barely-there hair, felt both invisible and exposed.

"Frankie? FRANKIE!"

The voice cut through the crowd noise, and heads turned. Of course they did. Because there was golden-haired Morgan Orr, pushing through the crowds like a man on a mission, wearing—

What was he wearing?

It looked like a traditional formal tunic, well fitted at shoulders and hips. But the fabric shifted color as he moved—now midnight blue, now silver, now something that didn't have a name. Light-reactive threads created patterns that responded to his gestures, making him look like a walking constellation. He looked like he'd fallen into a fashion fabricator and hit every button on the way down.

His tall, lanky frame gave him an advantage as he maneuvered through the crowd, those big dark eyes—almost cartoonishly expressive—scanning for her. His multi-hued blond waves were sculpted upward in a style that defied both gravity and good sense. Gold dust wasn't just in his hair but dusted across his high cheekbones, complementing the subtle geometric patterns traced in metallic ink that extended from the corners of his eyes—more restrained than the kohl, but somehow more effective for it.

He looked both exhausted, wired on stimulants, and genuinely delighted to see her.

Unfortunately.

"What are you doing here?" Frankie said.

"Waiting for you!"

Spike had moved to the other side of Frankie, perhaps because of the delicious meat smells coming from a nearby kiosk.

"But how did you know to be here? I didn't even tell you I was coming."

"Spike did. But she didn't say when."

They both glowered down at the unrepentant cyvlossic; Morgan mad about the missing detail, Frankie mad because what the heck?

"So I came early," Morgan prattled on, like a music station announcer who was vamping while trying to start up the next song. "Plus, I needed a quiet place to finish my thesis. I think I've memorized the entire thing. Also, I think I've developed a caffeine dependency. Did you know they have forty-seven varieties of coffee here now? I've tried them all. Twice."

"Morgan—"

"Your hair! Quite decisive. Very 'I don't care about your beauty standards.' That slope is actually coming into style in the underground clubs. Not that I go to underground clubs. Anymore. Recently."

He paused, seeming to realize he was babbling, and ran his fingers through both sides of his hair simultaneously, somehow managing not to disturb its sculptural perfection.

"Hi," he said.

Despite everything, Frankie felt a smile tugging at her lips. "Hi."

They stood there for a moment, uncertainty crackling between them. Then Morgan made a formal Cooperative bow—perfect form, exact angle for greeting a peer—before catching himself halfway through.

"Sorry, I—reflex—"

Frankie found herself automatically returning the bow before she could stop herself, hands in the correct position, spine at the proper angle. For a moment, they were two trained courtiers performing their roles. Frankie shivered.

Then Spike sneezed dramatically, breaking the moment.

"Does your creature require—" Morgan started.

"Training in manners? Yes."

Around them, the crowd's attention was shifting. She could feel it—the subtle turn of heads, the pauses in conversations. Morgan's appearance alone would draw eyes, but add in their perfect formal bows, her diplomatic clearance codes that security was probably gossiping about…

"We should move," she said quietly.

"Right. Yes. I have a transport reserved. Well, I've had one reserved for four days. They know me now. The transport dispatchers. We're on first-name basis. I may have overshared about my thesis." Morgan reached around her, tapping the floating luggage so it would follow him. He headed across the wide space, gesturing for them to follow. "It's about Outer World Integration Precedents. Chapter Three examines the sociological impact of—"

"Morgan."

"Right. Moving. Not talking about my thesis."

But he kept glancing at her as they walked, like he was checking she was really there. The exhaustion showed more clearly up close—shadows under his eyes that expensive concealer couldn't quite hide, a tremor in his hands from too much caffeine.

"You really didn't have to come," Frankie said softly.

"Yes, I did." For a moment, his manic energy stilled. "Coming back here… I remember what it was like. The first time. After." He didn't need to specify after what. "It's good to see a friendly face. Someone who knew you before. Someone who gets it."

Frankie's throat tightened. She'd been so focused on her own anxiety, she'd forgotten. Morgan had his own complicated history with Zichi. The golden son who'd never quite fit the mold. Who'd left for the outer worlds and came back changed.

"Besides," he added, the manic brightness returning, "where

else would I get to wear this?" He gestured at his light-show outfit. "It's fresh from the designer. Not even in stores yet. I'm a walking advertisement for questionable choices."

"You look like a dance club achieved sentience."

"Yes!"

They reached the transport hub for the inner rings, and Morgan waved his hand over a scanner. Premium access, of course. A private capsule slid up to the platform. Its doors opened with expensive silence onto a round room with tall windows and a semicircle of the most comfortable-looking reclining seats she'd ever seen.

"After you," Morgan said, then caught himself again. "Sorry, that's—we don't have to do the whole—"

"It's fine." Frankie stepped into the capsule, sinking into seats that adjusted automatically to support her spine. The familiar luxury made her skin crawl. "We're going to be swimming in etiquette for the next two weeks. Might as well start practicing."

"Right. The wedding. Your friend. The Regent. Formal dinners where everyone pretends they're not dissecting your every gesture."

"You're really selling it."

Spike flowed into the capsule last, claiming a seat with regal disdain.

The doors sealed, and Morgan input their destination. CapCity.

"Shouldn't we hit your hotel? Get your stuff?"

"Family's got a condo on the base." Morgan shrugged. "And I've got my thesis right here." He tapped the tunic pocket over his heart.

The capsule began to move, accelerating smoothly toward the planet below. Through its wide windows, Zichi grew larger—that brown-red heart surrounded by its thin green ring of life.

"Home sweet home," Morgan said, but there was no sweetness in it.

Frankie watched the planet approach and tried not to think about all the reasons she'd sworn never to come back.

At least she wasn't doing it alone.

THE DESCENT through Zichi's atmosphere took forty-three minutes. Frankie knew because she counted each one, watching the planet's surface resolve from abstract patterns into geographic reality.

First came the oceans—that beautiful, deceptive blue that looked inviting until you knew better. The Cooperative had tried for centuries to make them useful, but Zichi's seas remained stubbornly hostile. Not wild like some worlds, just… unwelcoming. As if the planet itself had decided that land was for people and water was for whatever lurked beneath those pretty surfaces.

Then the continent emerged, and Frankie's breath caught despite herself. From this height, you could see the truth of Zichi laid bare: a massive brown wound of desert surrounded by a thin scab of green. The fertile ring looked impossibly narrow from up here, a mere thread of habitability clinging to the coastline. How did four billion people fit in that space?

Vertically, she reminded herself. They built up because they couldn't build in.

"Look," Morgan said, pointing to the northeast quadrant. "Sandstorm season's starting early."

A red-brown haze obscured part of the desert interior, a wall of sand that looked solid as stone from this distance. Even with all their technology, the Cooperative couldn't stop the desert from trying to reclaim its territory.

"My sinuses are already protesting," Frankie muttered.

"Wait until you smell the climate control systems. They've 'improved' them." Morgan made air quotes. "Now everything smells like chalk."

Spike stretched across her bench, playing up the languid pet routine. Only Frankie caught the way her eyes tracked their descent, calculating angles and distances with predator precision.

The capsule banked, following the prescribed approach vector for Capital District. Below them, the city emerged from the coastal haze like something from a fever dream. Towers of white and silver rose in precise patterns, each building exactly where it should be, no sprawl, no chaos, no organic growth. Just planned perfection stretching up and up and up.

"Regent's Complex," Morgan said, pointing to a sprawl of green and gold that looked obscene against the vertical city. "Only horizontal gardens in the district. Well, besides the other First Families' estates, but none of them are quite so..."

"Ostentatiously wasteful?"

"I was going to say 'historically significant,' but yours works too."

The capsule began its final descent, and Frankie could make out individual buildings now. Media screens covered every available surface, turning the city into a glittering info-hazard. Even from here, she could see the news cycling through—trade agreements, cultural events, who wore what to which gala.

"Is that—" She leaned forward, squinting at one of the larger screens.

Her. At the last commemoration event.

"Oh, that." Morgan sounded embarrassed. "Yeah, there's been some coverage. Your Beth's marrying the Regent's son—it's news, right? They've been running retrospectives on the Orphans of Wala. You might want to... avoid the screens for a bit."

A PSA flashed beside her: "Your tax-credits at work—saving

outer-world orphans since the Wala Tragedy." Still milking that photo, two decades later.

Frankie's stomach dropped. Of course. Should have expected this. The prodigal orphan returns for the wedding of the decade. A media feast.

"How bad?"

"They're using your old publicity photos. The ones where you're nineteen and wearing that terrible gray dress with the—"

"With the ruffles." She put a hand over her eyes as if that would block the memory. Undergraduate commencement. What a nightmare.

"The feed is forever." Morgan paused. "They've been kind, mostly. Focusing on Beth's 'fairy tale ending' and glossing over the rest."

Spike made a low growl. Frankie agreed. Fairy tale narratives were some kind of bullshit.

Their ears popped once more, and then the capsule was touching down with barely a whisper, settling onto a platform that jutted out from Terminal Five—the diplomatic quarter. Of course Morgan would have clearance for the fancy terminal.

"Ready?" he asked, hand hovering over the door release.

"No," Frankie said. "But that's never stopped me before."

The doors slid open, and Capital City air hit her like a physical force. Morgan hadn't been wrong about the smell—something chalky, something chemical that probably had a three-page name and was designed to keep everyone calm and compliant.

And underneath it, sneaking through the climate control's best efforts, the ghost of desert sand.

Just off the platform, a woman in Regent blue and cream livery stood waiting by a bubble car, a sleek miniature of the capsule they'd come down in.

"Citizen Styles? I'm here to escort you to the Complex. The Regent extends her warmest welcome home."

Frankie didn't correct the title. What was the point? Here, she'd always be Citizen Styles, Ward of the Regent, Orphan of Wala. Her trader's clothes and wild hair couldn't change that.

"Thank you," she managed, falling back on trained politeness.

The woman's eyes flicked to Spike with barely concealed alarm. "Your… companion… has been cleared for entry. Distinguished Citizen Blais told me of your preference for cyvlossic companionship."

Preference. As if Spike were an accessory.

"The Regent wishes to ensure your complete comfort during your stay."

Her stay. Like she was visiting, not trapped by obligation.

Morgan touched her elbow lightly. "I'll ride with you. Staying at the family pile. After I blew the first thesis review, they revoked my dorm privileges." He grinned. "Thought that would stop me. Hah!"

They glided through the vertical city on magnetic lines, silent and smooth. Buildings rose on either side like canyon walls, connected by bridges that looked like spider silk from below. People moved on multiple levels—walkways, tubes, aerial platforms—all in perfect patterns that kept traffic flowing.

"Population's up another three percent," Morgan said, making conversation. "They're talking about building higher. Some of the towers are already pumping oxygen into their upper reaches."

Frankie watched a family on a mid-level walkway, the children in miniature versions of their parents' formal wear. The precise way they moved, the careful distances they maintained. Everything choreographed by a lifetime of training.

"Still avoiding the desert?" she asked.

"More than ever. They've declared another fifty kilometers 'protected zone.' For environmental reasons, supposedly, but really…"

"Really they're scared of it."

"Can you blame them? Last year a storm broke through the barriers in Sector 7. Buried three blocks before they got it contained. Nobody died, but the cleanup took months."

Frankie remembered to breathe. With every block closer to the Regent's Complex, she felt like she'd lost another year of her life. Already she felt twelve again, dressed in royal blue and cream and grateful for any scrap of belonging.

Morgan put his hand over hers. Solid, grounding, even if his skin did shimmer with golden powder.

"How's Celine?" Frankie asked.

Morgan's hand flinched, but did not leave Frankie's "Fantastic! She's brilliant, you know. Her thesis was approved almost before she finished it." He sighed. "She's apprenticing with a family lawyer her dad knows, and trying to figure out if she wants more education now, or later."

"And... you two?"

Now the hand left hers and went to gently stroke Morgan's neck. "Great, great. She got me through the first year. You know there are dozens of different ways to study?"

The Regent's courier, sitting in front, had to hide a smile.

"But then she wouldn't help me at all on the thesis. 'Not interested in that kind of law,' she said." He shrugged, making his tunic swirl. "And now that I'm staying at home, she won't even come visit if my brother is there. And he lives there!"

"Do you blame her?"

"Well, he *is* a prig, and oh so full of himself, to be sure. But he can't really hurt her—we don't even have a water feature here! Nothing for David to 'accidentally' push her into. And," Morgan leaned closer, speaking low. "I think she could take him now, in a fight."

The transport curved around a final bend, and there they were: the gates of the Complex. Ancient stone and modern force fields, just like she remembered. The biometric scanners were new, though, sweeping the transport with invisible fingers.

"Welcome home, Francesca Styles," the gate system announced in warm, cultured tones. "The Regent is delighted by your return."

The words hit her like a slap. Not Fridrika. Francesca. The name they'd given her when she arrived, scared and grieving and alone. The name that meant "you belong to us now."

The name she'd given them back in a screaming fit when she was sixteen. Like that was going to work.

The transport slid through the gates, into gardens that sprawled horizontally in defiance of everything the vertical city represented. Real earth. Real plants. Real space to breathe.

Real cage.

"I can't," Frankie heard herself say.

Morgan took her hand. Spike brushed her leg, warm and soft.

She looked at Morgan's face, weary and warm and not chiaroscuro like his clothing currently was.

"Stay a bit?"

"Of course."

The transport stopped at the main entrance, an ancient stone gate protected by a great glass cube of a building. Through the clear walls, Frankie could see people in blue and cream, waiting. Behind them, the wide wooden doors to her past stood open, spilling golden light onto ancient stones.

The transport's door slid open. Frankie took a breath that tasted of chalk and sand and secrets.

She stepped out.

CHAPTER
FOUR

THE VAST, deep entrance hall of the Regent's Complex hadn't changed. That was the first thing that hit Frankie, harder than the processed air or the perfect temperature. All these years, and not a single ornament, chair, rug—anything—had been moved.

The same impossible acoustics that made whispers carry to the vaulted ceiling while footsteps vanished into nothing. The same light patterns embedded in the polished wood floor—blue for public areas, gold for private, red for restricted.

Even the smell was the same. Or rather, the absence of smell. The Complex's air was scrubbed down to nothing, like breathing distilled water. It made her sinuses ache and her throat feel coated with chalk.

"Citizen Styles." The voice made her freeze. For a moment, she was thirteen again, caught sneaking back from the gardens after curfew. But when she turned, it wasn't Proctor Lizbet.

It was worse. It was Proctor Lizbet's philosophical twin, down to the steel-gray hair pulled back in the same unforgiving bun, the same ramrod posture, the same pursed lips.

"I am Proctor Merin Satch," the woman continued in High

Galactic, each syllable precise as a blade. "I have the honor of overseeing the Complex's protocols."

"Proctor," Frankie managed, her body automatically performing the shallow bow appropriate for greeting a senior staff member. Her hands folded into the correct position without conscious thought—left over right, fingers aligned, with the clench of her stomach an added bonus.

Proctor Merin's eyes—the same shade of judgment as Lizbet's —swept over them with clinical efficiency. Frankie in her trader clothes, Morgan in his light-show disaster, Spike a tornado of tufted fur.

"Your… companion animal," the Proctor said, making it sound like a sexually transmitted disease, "has been cleared for access. However, I must remind you that the Complex maintains certain standards."

"Of course," Frankie said. The old phrases came back like muscle memory. "I appreciate the accommodation."

"The Regent extends her warmest welcome," Proctor Merin continued, though her tone suggested the Regent's warmth and the Proctor's were entirely different temperatures. "She regrets that pressing matters prevent her from greeting you personally. As does Distinguished Citizen Blais, who is engaged with wedding preparations."

As they began walking, Frankie's feet found the patterns in the floor without conscious thought. Blue line to gold intersection, angle left at the portrait of the Third Regent. Her body knew this place the way it knew how to breathe.

They passed the portrait hall, where former Regents gazed down with painted disappointment. Each gilt frame might as well have been a tombstone: Here Lies One More Ruler Willing to Use an Eight-Year-Old Girl as Proof of Good Governance.

The formal dining hall appeared through an archway—just a glimpse, but the sight of it kicked open doors to too many memories. That table that could seat two hundred fifty, the chandeliers designed to make hiding expressions impossible. The savory smells of dinner prep seeping from the kitchens made bile rise in her throat.

Her hand moved automatically to where a dinner napkin would rest. Morgan caught the gesture, his fingers brushing her elbow. The touch grounded her, pulled her back to now.

Past the dining room hall, the gardens appeared through the hall's floor-to-ceiling windows, and Frankie's breath caught. Obscene luxury—horizontal space stretching for acres while the vertical city clawed skyward for every meter.

They entered the former ward wing through a gray stone archway that tried to be welcoming. The corridors were smaller here, the ceilings lower. The smell changed too—a little perfume, a little polish, the faintest trace of actual life.

"Your quarters," Proctor Merin announced, stopping before a pale wood door that looked like all the others in the spare white hall. She pressed her hand to the scanner embedded beside it, and it opened inward silently. "The Regent felt you would appreciate privacy during your stay."

The suite beyond was excessive, and Frankie's first breath of it tasted wrong. Too purified, too perfect, like it had been focus-grouped and optimized for maximum inoffensiveness.

The sitting room sprawled before her in an irregular pentagon, designed to feel organic while being anything but. The ceiling soared to at least four meters, creating a sense of openness that somehow made her feel smaller. Pale gold walls caught the afternoon light filtering through those floor-to-ceiling windows that dominated two of the five walls, meeting at an angle that showcased both the gardens and a slice of the city beyond.

Every surface gleamed with that particular Complex sheen— not quite matte, not quite glossy, but something in between that made her eyes slide off edges. The color palette whispered wealth: cream carpets, walls in that subtle gold, furniture in shades of ivory and sand with strategic touches of deep blue and burgundy. Like someone had taken the concept of "expensive neutral" and weaponized it.

The carpet under her boots was thick enough to swallow footsteps, a shade that would show every speck of dirt if dirt were allowed to exist here. It felt like walking on clouds, if clouds were designed to make you constantly aware of your own weight and unworthiness to tread on them.

The furniture arrangement created distinct zones without walls. To her immediate right, a conversation area: two of those deep ivory and blue loveseats facing each other across a low table that looked carved from a single piece of pale stone. Beyond that, near the angled windows, a dining space with a round table in honey-colored wood surrounded by six chairs upholstered in that same midnight silk. A kitchen alcove tucked into the far left corner, all gleaming surfaces and hidden appliances.

"Special accommodations have been made for your companion," the Proctor continued, indicating a corner where a window walls met a solid wall, to the side of the dining table. Someone had installed what looked like a luxury pet palace—cushions in graduated sizes from small to cyvlossic-sized, climbing structures that belonged in a museum, even a small fountain that burbled both unobtrusively and insistently. The whole setup positioned to catch both morning and afternoon sun.

Spike padded over to investigate, peering at every surface with the kind of focused attention she usually reserved for potential threats. She sniffed each cushion deliberately—the burgundy velvet, the cream cashmere, the blue silk that matched the loveseats. She tested a climbing post with one paw, its surface covered in what looked like hand-woven rope. Then she looked at the fountain with an expression that clearly said "you have got to be kidding me."

Then Spike turned her back on the entire setup and jumped onto the nicest piece of furniture in the room—a loveseat upholstered in hand-woven silk in a shade of blue so deep it was almost black. She circled twice, kneaded the fabric with her claws (Frankie could hear the delicate threads popping), and settled in. The contrast was magnificent: matted gray-orange-black fur against silk that probably required specialist cleaning.

Proctor Merin inhaled sharply, but said nothing.

"Beautiful space," Frankie said. "I appreciate the accommodation."

"Yes," Proctor Merin said, visibly collecting herself. "The Regent requests your presence at tonight's formal dinner."

"Tonight?" Frankie's voice shot up an octave.

"It's on your calendar," Proctor Merin said.

Frankie checked her wristcom. There it was. Shit. Must've missed that message during disembarkation or something. She read down the list of events she had not agreed to attend.

"Garden party?"

Morgan snorted. "Least of your problems."

"Tomorrow, yes," the proctor said. "Much bigger affair, but less formal." Proctor Merin stepped toward the bedroom archway —Frankie could glimpse the space beyond, more cream and gold, a bed that looked like a small continent. "You'll find a range of appropriate attire in the two wardrobes in your bedroom. The Distinguished said you're of a size. We'll send a tailor to finish you a half-hour before each event."

"Wonderful," Frankie said flatly.

Merin frowned at Frankie. "Your hair. Should we bring a wigmaker instead of a hairdresser?"

Ugh. Frankie ran a hand through the long ends of her short haircut, pushing the bangs to the side again. This cut was so easy. But nothing here was meant to be easy. "Not sure. What is the style etiquette these days?"

Proctor Merin pursed her lips. "I'll send both. But you might get away with the short, if we top it with a tiara or a tilt-chapeau. You are an Original, after all." She said it like it was a fatal disease.

"Thank you," Frankie said. "That's very considerate."

"Yes. I'll leave you to settle in." She moved with a grace that must have taken a decade to learn. She paused as the door swung open. "Welcome home, Citizen Styles."

The door closed with expensive silence, and Frankie stood very still, letting the room's overwhelming perfection wash over her. Now that she was alone—well, alone with Morgan and Spike —she could really take it in.

The windows didn't just show the gardens; they were positioned to frame specific views like living paintings. Through the left window, the formal rose gardens with their geometric precision. Through the right, a carefully wild grove that was supposed to look natural but probably required a phalanx of gardeners to maintain its studied casualness.

The light was somehow both natural and not, filtered through smart glass that adjusted its tint based on the sun's position. Right now it created a golden glow that made everything look like it was filmed through honey. Even the air seemed to glow, dust motes turned into tiny stars by whatever the glass was doing to the light.

To her right, through that archway, she glimpsed more of the bedroom. Not just a bed like a continent but an entire sitting area beyond it, and what might be a door to a private balcony. The cream-honey-gold theme continued there, punctuated by more of that midnight blue in throws and pillows arranged with mathematical precision.

To her left, the kitchen gleamed like a surgical suite. Frankie moved closer, running her hand along the counter—some kind of composite that felt warm to the touch, neither stone nor synthetic but something in between. The appliances hid behind panels that matched the walls perfectly. You'd never know there was a cold storage unit until you pressed the right spot and it whispered open.

Everything smelled like nothing. That was still the worst part. Even the Spear's recycled air had character—hints of engine oil, coffee, Spike's fur, the ghost of whatever they'd cooked last. This air was aggressively neutral, temperature-controlled to the degree, humidity-adjusted, particle-filtered until it barely felt like air at all. It made her feel like she wasn't quite real, like she might dissolve into the same perfect nothing if she stayed still too long.

"Breathe," Morgan said gently.

She hadn't realized she'd stopped. The exhale came out shaky.

"It's like living inside a medical facility," she said, moving deeper into the room. Even her voice seemed muffled, contained, controlled. "Everything designed to prevent contamination."

"Including contamination by actual life," Morgan agreed. He'd found the room's control panel set discreetly into the wall near the kitchen—of course it was near the kitchen, maximum efficiency—and was poking at it with the dedication of someone solving a puzzle. "Look at this. You can adjust the window opacity, the air flow, the temperature in half-degree increments. You can even—oh."

A soft chime, and a section of wall by the dining table opened to reveal a refreshment station. Not just any refreshment station—tiers of gleaming equipment that looked like it could produce anything from water to complex molecular cocktails.

"Is that…" Morgan moved closer, his ridiculous outfit shifting through excited patterns that clashed magnificently with the suite's studied elegance. "It is! A molecular gastronomy unit. Consumer grade, but still."

He started exploring with the enthusiasm of a child in a candy store, pulling out items that the station had apparently prestocked based on some algorithm of their assumed preferences. The inside was all clean white surfaces and subtle lighting, making the colorful food items look like jewelry in a display case.

"Look at this! Deconstructed fruit spheres. Emotion-responsive tea. And—"

He held up something that looked like a simple cream puff but shimmered slightly in the light, almost iridescent.

"Molecular reconstruction pastry. It's supposedly engineered at the atomic level to taste like perfect childhood memories." He bit into it, and his eyes went wide. "Oh. Oh, that's delicious. And disturbing. Tastes exactly like the cookies my grandmother made, but also like… achievement? Victory?"

He broke off half and offered it to her. "You have to try this."

Frankie took the piece reluctantly. The cream inside looked too perfect, too white, like it had never met actual dairy. She took a small bite, and—

Ice. Confusion. Terror.

She swallowed hard, forcing the bite down. The pastry tasted like loss. Like standing at a picture window on a crowded orbital station, eight years old, watching everything she'd ever known shrink to a point of light and disappear.

"What does it taste like to you?" Morgan asked.

"Winter." She walked over to the loveseat where Spike was sprawled in magnificent disdain. "Here, see what childhood memories a cyvlossic has."

She held out the rest of the pastry. Spike lifted her head, sniffed delicately, then deeper. The powdered sugar coating puffed up around her nose.

The sneeze was explosive. Sugar went everywhere—on the priceless silk, on Frankie's cargo pants, on the cream carpet. The half-eaten pastry flew from Frankie's hand and landed with a wet splat on the pristine coffee table. Spike sneezed again, and again, each one sending new clouds of sugar into the perfect air.

"Good kitty," Frankie said, scratching behind Spike's ears.

Morgan laughed, a real laugh that broke through his earlier performance. "I think she just improved the décor."

Frankie sank onto the loveseat next to Spike, the cushions adjusting automatically to support her spine in ways that felt a little too intimate.

The silk was cool against her palms. From here, the whole space looked different. The way the afternoon light pooled on the cream carpet, turning it golden. The subtle way the walls weren't quite straight but curved slightly, creating a sense of flow that kept drawing your eye around the room. Even the air currents had been designed—she could feel the faintest breeze from hidden vents, just enough to keep the air moving without ever feeling drafty.

Morgan had moved on to beverages, pulling out bulbs of liquids that glowed and shifted color. The molecular gastronomy unit cast colored light on his face as he explored, making him look like a kid at a carnival. "Mood-responsive hydration. It changes flavor based on your emotional state." He took a sip and made a face. "Tastes like curiosity mixed with mild anxiety. Accurate, but creepy."

The light from the windows was starting to shift, the smart glass adjusting its tint to maintain the perfect golden hour feeling even as the real golden hour faded. The gardens beyond took on deeper colors—emerald greens going to forest, the roses burning like coals in their geometric beds. Frankie could see the paths she used to escape down, each curve designed to create moments of reveal and concealment. The grove where she'd hide until Proctor Lizbet came to collect her, its "wildness" just as managed as everything else. Everything exactly as she'd left it, like the whole Complex had been held in stasis, waiting for its wayward children to return.

Her throat felt tight. The perfect air wasn't helping.

"This is what we gave up," she said quietly. "Rooms bigger than most people's homes. Food that reads your mind. Every comfort, as long as you—"

The door chimed.

Frankie's whole body tensed, that trained response to unexpected visitors no amount of years could erase. Morgan turned from his molecular experiments, a glowing drink in each hand— one shifting from blue to purple, the other pulsing pink.

"Come in," Frankie called, though she knew the visitor would enter regardless. She stood up, preparing herself. Girding herself.

The door slid open.

Beth stood in the doorway, a sun going supernova.

CHAPTER
FIVE

BETH STEPPED into the room like a slow-moving comet burning through the atmosphere. She absolutely glowed. The deep purple of her tunic should have made her look severe, but instead she looked like royalty from a fairy tale, the kind that grants wishes or curses with equal grace.

For a moment, neither of them moved. Frankie couldn't. Her body had forgotten how to breathe, how to stand, how to exist in the same space as this luminous creature who used to gossip and braid her hair in the dormitory bathroom.

And Beth's hair—great Safra. What had once hung in simple braids was now an architectural marvel that laughed at gravity. Twists and loops and spirals. Tiny gems woven through her dark as night hair caught the afternoon light from the windows and scattered it like stars. The style must have taken hours.

Her face had changed too. Fuller, stronger, with fine lines at the corners of her eyes that spoke of both laughter and long nights reading policy documents. Her cheekbones seemed sharper, or maybe that was just the way the Complex's perfect lighting loved her. The glow wasn't makeup—it came from within, as if joy had transformed her at a cellular level.

And she wore jewelry now. Geometric gold pieces that traced her collarbones like armor, caught at her wrists like delicate shackles. Each piece moved with her breathing, creating subtle music—the faint chime of privilege and power.

Beth's body started to shift into the start of a formal greeting. Her spine straightened even further—and how was that possible when she already stood like a dancer? Her hands started to position for the ceremonial bow between equals, fingers aligning with the precision of years of practice. Her weight transferred to her heels, allowing for a bow that showed respect without submission.

Then her face cracked. Not the polished political half-smile that had been hovering at the edges, but a grin so purely Beth that all the years collapsed into nothing.

Frankie, still frozen, braced for impact.

Beth flew across the room, her formal shoes silent on the thick carpet. The scent hit Frankie first—jasmine, but not the synthetic kind. Real jasmine, probably grown in the Complex gardens, probably picked at the exact moment of peak fragrance. Under it, something else. The phantom smell of cheap dormitory shampoo and late-night instant noodles and dreams bigger than either of them could hold.

The hug hit Frankie like a friendly meteor. Beth still hugged like she was trying to squeeze all her feelings through her arms, pulling Frankie so tight her ribs creaked. Her body was different—fuller, stronger, muscles under the silk. But the essence was the same. The little humming sound she made when she was happy. The way she rocked slightly side to side, as if the joy couldn't be contained in stillness.

"You're here," Beth whispered into her shoulder. Her breath was warm, real, present. "You're actually here."

"You're glowing," Frankie whispered back. "Actually glowing. Did you eat something radioactive?"

Beth laughed—that bright, uncontrolled sound that no amount of political training could polish away. It bubbled up from her chest and filled the perfect air with imperfection. She pulled back just enough to look at Frankie's face, and her hands came up to cup Frankie's cheeks. Her palms were soft and smelled faintly of some expensive lotion.

"Look at you." Beth's eyes traced Frankie's face like she was memorizing it. "Your hair is so wild! I love it. You look like yourself. Really yourself." Her eyes were bright with unshed tears, and this close, Frankie could see they'd gone from brown to amber, catching and holding light like expensive whiskey. "I've missed you. So much."

"Beth—"

"No, don't. You're here now. That's what matters."

She squeezed once more, and Frankie felt something in her chest crack open. This was Beth. Her Beth. The girl who'd held her hair back when she threw up from nerves before her first formal dinner. The girl who'd stolen extra desserts and hidden them in Frankie's room when she was too scared to go to the dining hall. The girl who'd promised they'd survive together or not at all.

Then Beth seemed to notice they weren't alone. The transformation was subtle but complete—her shoulders straightened a fraction more, her chin lifted, her eyes went from soft to assessing in a heartbeat. She turned, hands still on Frankie's arms, her touch now both affection and claim.

"Hello, Morgan."

Even her voice changed. Still warm, but with more layers now —assessment and calculation and forty different ways this conversation could go. She didn't release Frankie as she spoke, keeping her anchored like a prize or a prop or maybe just someone she couldn't bear to let go of.

Morgan had stood when she entered—proper etiquette—and now looked genuinely stunned. Powdered sugar decorated his chin.

"I—yes. Distinguished Citizen Blais. It is an honor." He managed to set down the two drinks he was holding while performing a perfectly respectful bow, despite the sugar. His outfit's lights flickered through muted, somewhat impressed patterns. "Your reputation precedes you."

"As does yours." Beth's tone was pleasant but carried edges sharp enough to cut glass. She released Frankie and glided forward—and it was gliding, each step calculated for maximum grace while appearing effortless. The silk of her tunic moved like water, revealing and concealing the strength underneath. "The paper you wrote on dialect preservation in the outer territories was fascinating. Though I disagreed with your conclusions about natural linguistic evolution."

She stopped at exactly the right distance—close enough for conversation, far enough to require him to come to her if he wanted to shake hands. Power positioning, as natural to her as breathing.

Morgan's eyes lit up. "You read my paper?"

"I read everything that might affect integration policy." Now Beth extended her hand—not for a formal touch but for an actual handshake. Another calculated choice. Treating him as an equal, or at least someone worth treating as an equal. "Your brother speaks highly of your academic work. He seems… surprised."

Her fingers were manicured now, Frankie noticed. Perfect ovals in a shade of pink that matched nothing and everything. The handshake was firm, brief, professionally warm.

"Ah. Well. David." Morgan mirrored the handshake, and

appeared to be recalibrating. He'd probably never seen the real Beth. Or, not the real Beth—Beth was always real—but the "inside" Beth. "He considers anything less than total political immersion to be failure."

"And you consider political immersion to be…?"

"Soul-crushing, generally." Morgan started to grin. "Present company excepted, of course."

Beth laughed—a political laugh this time, controlled and melodious, designed to make the listener feel clever without actually confirming that they were. "Of course. Frankie, I see why you like him."

She moved back to Frankie with the same gliding steps, linking their arms in a gesture so natural it made Frankie's chest tight. The silk of her sleeve was soft against Frankie's bare forearm. This time, this close, she could see the cleverly concealed bags under her eyes. Beth needed a rest.

Good luck with that.

"Yes," Frankie said, finding her voice again. "Morgan, you have sugar on your chin."

He wiped it away without embarrassment. "Occupational hazard of molecular gastronomy. Distinguished Blais, would you like to try? The flavor profile is extraordinary."

"Beth," she corrected, and even that was calculated—the gift of informality, handed out like candy to someone who might be useful. "And no thank you. I've been taste-testing wedding cakes all morning. If I eat another sweet thing, I might actually become one."

She guided them to the middle sofa with the unconscious authority of someone used to directing foot traffic, her hand on Frankie's elbow gentle but inexorable. Even sitting was graceful —she folded onto the cushions like origami, every angle perfect.

Frankie crowded Spike to find a place in the middle. The sofa, still trying to fix Frankie's posture, seemed to recognize a master and simply surrendered to Beth's already-perfect spine.

"Cakes?" Frankie asked. "The wedding's—"

"A week from tomorrow, yes, but tonight—" Beth's face lit up with what looked like genuine panic. "Oh, didn't you get the message? Tonight's the formal dinner. The small one. Well, small-ish. Proctor Merin was supposed to—"

"She mentioned it," Frankie admitted, stomach sinking. "I thought I'd have more time to—"

"I know, I know. It's awful timing. Everything's a crush, and it's the only slot that worked. If you'd been late…" She sighed. "But you weren't."

"You could say I was," Frankie said, hope creeping into her voice.

"Your arrival was noted on the media." Beth frowned, a real frown that taxed the fine powder over her cheeks. "Don't pay any attention to the media, okay?" She looked over at Morgan, who had seated himself on the opposite loveseat, his two bulbs of liquid experiment forgotten on the short table between them. "Morgan can tell you if you need to know any of it."

So it must be really bad.

"Great." Frankie said. "Can I at least listen to the new music?"

"And the old," Morgan said. He shook his wrist, signaling his wristcom to display a small floating screen. "I believe that band you like—Screaming Banshees?"

"Screeching Bananas."

"Yeah, them. They're here, doing a gig at the university stadium." He looked up at her conspiratorially. "But they always do a smaller one, somewhere secret. Want me to get us in?"

"Yes! Wait, no." Frankie looked at Beth, worried, pleading. "Can I?"

"What would Proctor Merin say?"

Frankie's face fell. Beth laughed her real laugh. "She'd say you're a grown woman. Do what you want, dummy."

"And face the consequences," Frankie said, mimicking their old proctor.

"Well, yes. But in this case there shouldn't be much." She glanced at Morgan. "If you go to the small one. And if it doesn't interfere with your schedule. Just put it on your calendar as 'private time,' and dare Proctor Merin to challenge it."

Morgan grinned. "I like your friend, Frankie. Beautiful, practical, devious."

"Taken," Beth said, grinning back. "So tonight, it won't be that bad. Easy re-entry. Forty or fifty people. Mostly family, a few ministers." She said it like forty or fifty of the most powerful people in Cooperative space was a casual gathering.

"Easy re-entry is you and me and your fiancé having a picnic in the garden," Frankie said.

"Oh, yes, you do have to meet Alain properly. You'll love him."

"Of course."

Beth didn't seem to hear. "He's brilliant, but so wonderfully oblivious to anything that isn't growing in dirt. Or water. Or air, actually—his new project involves floating gardens. Yesterday I found him in his lab at three in the morning because his singing orchids had developed harmonies and he wanted to record them."

"Singing orchids?" Morgan leaned forward, genuinely interested. His mother was an agricultural artist.

"His latest success. He's crossing Twilight phosphorescent flora with Cloud orchids. They sing at different frequencies based on light exposure. It's actually quite beautiful, if you like alien plant music at dawn." She said it with the fond exasperation of someone who'd probably been woken by alien plant music more than once.

"And you do?" Frankie asked.

Beth's face softened into something private, young, unguarded. "I like him. It's... he gets so excited about his discoveries. Like a kid with a new toy. Last month he made roses that change color with your mood. Completely impractical, terrible for security, but he was so proud. He gave me a bouquet and they went through the entire spectrum in about five seconds. Apparently I have complicated feelings about roses."

She laughed at herself, and it was real Beth-laughter, not the political version. But then something shifted in her expression, like clouds crossing the sun.

"His family thinks he's weak. Too soft for politics. Too interested in beauty instead of power." Her voice hardened. "They can't see that creating beauty in this world is another form of power. That making something grow where nothing should grow is the greatest rebellion."

The vehemence surprised Frankie. This was new—Beth defending someone else's gentleness instead of trying to forge them into something harder.

"Anyway," Beth continued, visibly collecting herself. "It's come up. There was an... incident. Lucien was almost killed."

"Assassination attempt?" Frankie was shocked.

"Security determined it was an accident." Beth said. "He fell down a hole. Don't ask. Luckily, it wasn't at a public event, just a small garden party. Anyway, it's made people look closer at the family dynamics. And nobody wants Alain for their regent, least of all Alain."

Spike's ears perked up at that. The cyvlossic was only pretending to sleep.

Was this the "unusual behavior" Bruce wanted them to look out for? What did this mean for Beth? Was she in danger, too?

Frankie's thoughts started to spin. Of course, Beth had security at the Complex. But so did Lucien, being the heir and all. And someone got to him. Almost.

"Now tell her the good part," Morgan said quickly. "The part that knocked the wedding off the top of the feed for two days."

"The Regent announced that there's a third son. Raised quietly outside the capital. Away from all… this." She gestured at the perfect room, the calculated luxury. "Fully adult, fully trained. And not owing anything to any of the Great Houses."

What a coup, so to speak. Regents had had "quiet children" in past generations. But it was so much harder when the Regent was actually the one to give birth to them.

"So now everybody wants Lucien healthy, because at least they know where he stands," Beth continued. "And now Alain's free to marry who he wants and grow his singing flowers and never have to pretend to care about trade negotiations. Everyone wins."

"Everyone?" Frankie asked quietly.

Beth's hand tightened on her arm. "Everyone who matters to me."

The political Beth was back, just that quick. Drawing lines between who mattered and who didn't, calculating advantage even in love.

Or maybe because of love.

"Speaking of people who matter," Beth continued, looking past Frankie. "Are you going to introduce me to your new friend? And tell me where in the worlds you got your hands on a tame cyvlossic."

Spike cracked an eye open.

"Beth, this is Spike." Frankie made the hand sign to show Spike was a girl. "My companion animal." Spike lifted her head, disreputably regal.

"She's magnificent." Beth studied Spike, who looked back at her with studied coolness. "I've been trying to get approval for emotional support animals in the youth dormitories. The Proctors insist they're unsanitary."

"She's right," Frankie said. "Spike is many things. Completely sanitary isn't one of them."

Spike made a sound somewhere between a meow and a growl.

"That means she likes you," Frankie said, hoping it was true.

"Perfect. I'll cite her as an example of why rigid standards don't work." Beth squeezed Frankie's arm, her fingers finding the exact pressure point that said 'I'm here' without leaving marks. "See? You're helping already."

The casual assumption that Frankie would want to help with Complex politics made something twist in her gut. But Beth was already moving on, words flowing like water finding its course.

"The Regent is thrilled you're here. She wants to welcome you properly tonight. She—" Beth paused. "She understands why you left. Why you stayed away. But she's glad you came back. For this."

"For you," Frankie corrected.

"Yes." Beth's eyes went soft again. "I know it's hard. I know what it costs you to be here."

Morgan cleared his throat. "I could help Frankie. With protocol review, I mean. If you'd like. Since I'm here anyway and presumably not invited…"

He let it hang, the question implicit. Beth's eyes narrowed slightly, and Frankie could practically see the calculations spinning behind them. Morgan Orr. Second son. Academic. Here with Frankie. Useful? Threatening? Both?

"The Orr family received their invitation weeks ago," she said carefully. "David confirmed for himself and a guest. Your parents sent regrets."

"Of course they did." Morgan's smile didn't reach his eyes.

"Well, David does love a society wedding. All those opportunities for gossip."

"But you're here," Beth observed. "Now."

"Well, you know. Friends don't let friends face their past alone."

Beth looked between them, and Frankie could see her reevaluating, adding new data to whatever massive mental spreadsheet she maintained. Then she smiled—a real smile, not a political one.

"No," she said. "They don't." She stood in one fluid motion, somehow making it look like the room reorganized itself around her rather than the other way around. The purple silk settled into new patterns, each fold perfect. "Morgan, you will join us tonight. I'll have Proctor Merin add you to the list. Consider it thanks for supporting our girl."

Our girl. Like Frankie was still shared property of the Complex. But the casual inclusion of Morgan was so essentially Beth—gathering people, making connections, building networks of loyalty with every breath.

"That's very generous," Morgan said, standing as well.

"It's strategic," Beth corrected. "Having an Orr who actually likes Frankie at the table changes the dynamics. Plus, you can keep her from bolting when the fish course arrives. She always hated the formal fish course."

"Still do," Frankie muttered, letting Beth pull her to her feet. Standing, she could smell the starch in Beth's formal tunic, see the way the fabric had been pressed into submission.

"I know." Beth hugged her again, softer this time. This hug was different—not the collision of reunion but something more careful, as if she was memorizing the feel of it. "I know this is hard. Being here. Seeing everyone. But I'm so grateful you came. It wouldn't be right without you."

She pulled back, hands on Frankie's shoulders. "I have to run.

The florist is having a crisis about pollen counts and inter-world allergen policies. But we'll talk properly tonight, after dinner. Like old times. My suite has a balcony where they can't monitor. We can be real there."

"Beth—"

"Wear something in jewel tones. The blue, if they gave you the blue. They're photographing everything for the archives, and you look amazing in deep colors. No gray. Never gray." She kissed Frankie's cheek, leaving the faint trace of jasmine and lip gloss. Then she surprised Morgan by kissing his cheek as well. "Thank you. For getting her here. For staying."

She swept toward the door, then paused. In that moment, with the afternoon light catching her from behind, she looked like a painting. Something titled "Duty and Desire" or maybe just "The Price."

"Oh, and Frankie? The others—I know most of them aren't coming. I understand. I do. But it still…"

"I'll call them," Frankie promised. "After dinner. Tomorrow. I'll explain."

"You don't have to explain. Just… tell them I miss them. Tell them I know we all made different choices, but I still…" She stopped, political polish cracking completely. "Just tell them I love them. Whatever they think of me now."

Then she was gone, The room felt smaller without her in it, like she'd taken some essential energy with her when she left.

Morgan sat back down heavily. "Well. She's…"

"Yeah."

"I mean, the political analysis was razor-sharp, but also…"

"Yeah."

"Does she ever stop? Just… stop?"

Frankie sank into the sofa, suddenly exhausted. She should take a nap before the dinner gauntlet. "She used to. We'd sneak out to the gardens after lights-out and just lie in the grass. She'd tell me about her plans to change the system from inside. Make it more fair. More just. She really believed she could."

"And now?"

"Now she's doing it. Just… the cost…"

Spike rolled off the sofa and padded toward the bedroom. If the cyvlossic got there first, she'd claim the best pillow. Get her fur all over it.

Three hours to transform into Citizen Styles. Three hours to remember protocols she'd spent more than a decade forgetting. Three hours to prepare for forty of the Cooperative's finest to dissect her every move.

"I should go," Morgan said, but didn't move. "Let you prepare. Let me prepare! Have you practiced your grateful ward smile."

"I don't remember how," Frankie admitted.

"It's like this." He demonstrated—a smile that engaged no actual facial muscles above the mouth, eyes distant and properly respectful. "With a little head tilt that says 'I'm listening' when you're actually planning escape routes."

Despite everything, Frankie laughed. "You've been to these dinners."

"Oh, so many. David used to drag me as his plus-one before he started wife-shopping. Said it was good for me to see how real politics worked." He stood, finally, brushing sugar from his still-shifting outfit. "I'll be back in two hours. Make sure the tailor gets your hem right. Then we can walk down together. Face the firing squad as a unit."

"You don't have to—"

"Please refer to my previous remarks about friends," he said officiously. And then grinned. "Besides, I need to plan my outfit. Something that says 'reformed black sheep' but also 'surprisingly useful political game piece.' It's a delicate balance."

After he left, Frankie tried to rest in the gigantic bed. Tried to reconcile the Beth she'd held with the Beth who calculated political advantages between breaths. Both were real. Both were true.

And in an hour and a half, she'd be asked to do the same.

"What do you think?" she asked Spike, who had indeed colonized the fluffiest pillow. At least there were three other pillows between them. "Can we survive a formal dinner?"

Spike shrugged.

"That's what I thought," Frankie said, and went to find something jewel-toned to wear to her own execution.

CHAPTER
SIX

THE JEWEL-TONED dress felt like armor made of water.

Frankie stood in front of the suite's floor-length mirror while the tailor—a woman with hands like hummingbirds—made final adjustments. The dress was deep emerald, the color of old forests, and it sighed with her when she breathed. Which wasn't often, because the bodice was doing things to her ribs that definitely violated several humanitarian treaties.

"Perfect," the tailor murmured around a mouthful of pins. "Distinguished Citizen Blais has excellent taste."

Of course Beth had chosen this. It was exactly what Frankie would look best in, and damn the discomfort. The fabric whispered against itself with every movement, announcing her presence before she could even speak. The neckline was modest by Zichi standards—which meant it showed her collarbones and nothing else—but the way it draped made her look like she belonged here.

That was the worst part.

"Your hair," the hairdresser said from behind her. She was younger than the tailor, with the kind of aggressively cheerful energy that suggested she'd had experience dealing with difficult clients. "Short can be very striking. Very modern."

"Or very service class," the tailor muttered.

The hairdresser shot her a look that could have stripped paint. "Fashion is cyclical. What was servant becomes statement." She produced something that looked like a cross between a tiara and a weapon. "This will help."

The hairpiece was delicate silver, designed to rest just past her forehead and sweep back. The angle complemented the sharp angle cut of her hair. When the hairdresser finished placing it, Frankie looked… different. Not like herself, but not quite like Citizen Styles either. Something in between.

"There," the hairdresser said with satisfaction. "Now you look like someone who chose to cut their hair, not someone who couldn't afford to keep it long."

The door chimed before Frankie could decide if that was an insult.

"It's open," she called.

Morgan swept in, and Frankie had to bite her lip to keep from laughing.

He wore formal blacks—traditional, conservative, appropriate. Except the fabric seemed to be having an argument with itself about what color black actually was. It shifted from midnight to charcoal to something that might have been very dark purple, creating patterns that made her eyes water if she looked too long.

"Too much?" he asked, spreading his arms. The movement sent ripples of color—or non-color—cascading across the jacket.

"It's like someone weaponized subtlety," Frankie said.

"Exactly what I was going for. Reformed black sheep, but make it pop." He paused, taking her in. "You look—"

"Like I'm about to be sacrificed to the gods of commerce?"

"I was going to say formidable. That color makes you look like you could murder someone and make it seem like a gift." He glanced at the hairdresser and tailor, who were packing up their supplies with the efficiency of people who knew when to disappear. "Ready for this?"

"No."

"Good. Confidence would worry me." He waited until the staff left, then moved closer. His voice dropped. "Remember, you don't have to prove anything to anyone. You survived this place once. You're just visiting now."

"With forty of the Cooperative's most powerful people watching my every move."

"Forty-three, actually. I got the updated list." He produced a small tablet from somewhere—his jacket seemed to have pockets that existed in several dimensions. "Want to review who's who?"

"Will it help or make me more nervous?"

"Both, probably."

Frankie took a breath that the dress barely allowed. "Hit me."

"Minister Chen-Okoye—agriculture. She's Beth's future in-law's cousin. Apparently grows orchids that taste like memories, which sounds terrifying. Senator Voss—military contracts, thinks the border conflicts are just good business. First Citizen Bellemont—she owns half the media networks and remembers everything. First Nakamura—banking, follows money like it's a religion. And approximately thirty-seven other people who think dinner is a blood sport."

"And the Regent?"

Morgan's shifting jacket stilled for a moment. "She'll arrive precisely when it causes maximum impact. Usually between the second and third courses. Just enough time for everyone to wonder if she's coming, not long enough for anyone to relax."

They left the suite and walked through corridors that Frankie's feet remembered better than her mind. Left at the portrait of the Third Regent. Right at the junction with the gold lines. Her body fell into the proper pace—not too fast (eager), not too slow (reluctant), but the measured stride of someone who belonged.

"You're taking this better than I expected," Morgan said.

"Than you expected, or than I expected?" Frankie adjusted the formal collar without fighting it. Ten years ago, she would have been clawing at the fabric by now.

"Much better. I'm starting to worry you've been replaced by a protocol droid."

The dining room announced itself before they reached it—the sound of controlled conversation, the clink of expensive glass, the particular quality of air that had been perfumed and climate-controlled into submission. Frankie's hand reached for an invisible dinner napkin.

Morgan caught the gesture. "Want to review fish course protocols?"

"I want to run."

"Can't. These shoes weren't made for running." He lifted one foot to show off footwear that seemed to be made entirely of good intentions and architectural ambition. "Plus, Spike would never forgive us if we didn't bring back food."

The dining room doors were open—of course they were, closed doors implied exclusion and the Regent never excluded, only selectively included. A staff member in cream and gold stood at the threshold, tablet in hand.

"Citizen Francesca Styles and Citizen Morgan Orr," Morgan announced before they could be asked.

The woman's eyes flicked to her tablet, then to Frankie's hair, then back to her tablet. "Of course. The Bride's table, seats seventeen and eighteen."

The Bride's table. Because even here, even now, everything revolved around Beth's wedding.

They entered the dining room, and Frankie's breath caught. Not because it was beautiful—though it was, in that aggressive way the Complex had of making beauty into a weapon. But because it was exactly, precisely, the same as when she'd left.

The table could seat two hundred, though tonight only forty-three places were set. Each setting was a small city of crystal and silver, plates nested like flowers, glasses arranged in formation. The centerpieces were architectural marvels of plants with flowers that had been bred to have no scent. Wouldn't want to interfere with the food, after all.

The chandeliers above were programmed to cast light that made everyone look their best while making it impossible to hide expressions. The walls were covered in mirrors that weren't quite mirrors, creating infinite reflections of wealth and power and really excellent tailoring.

"Frankie!"

She turned to find Alain diCimino bearing down on her with the enthusiasm of a golden retriever who'd just discovered opposable thumbs. He was tall and loose-limbed, with the kind of tan that came from actually being outdoors rather than from a spa. His formal wear looked slightly wrong on him, like he'd borrowed it from someone who cared about clothes.

She didn't know him well. He was just enough older than them that it had made a difference when they were kids, and been away at schools most of the time, anyway.

"Beth said you'd come! This is magnificent. Have you seen the centerpieces? They're Twilight orchids crossed with something from Earth—roses, I think? They sing if you breathe on them just right. Here, try—"

"Alain." Beth materialized at his elbow, every inch the political player in another shade of deep purple shot with silver that made the fabric look liquid. But her smile when she looked at him was real. "Don't make Frankie breathe on the flowers before dinner. It's not proper."

"Nothing about singing flowers is proper," Alain said cheerfully. "That's what makes them interesting. Did you know they harmonize? I've been working on getting them to do rounds, but so far they only know two songs and one of them is apparently obscene in High Galactic."

Despite everything, Frankie found herself smiling. "Which one?"

"I'm not sure. No one will tell me. They just blush and change the subject." He leaned in conspiratorially. "I think it might be the one about pollination."

"Alain studies botanical genetics," Beth explained, though her fond exasperation suggested this was like saying the ocean studied being wet. "He's revolutionizing agricultural yields on seven planets."

"By accident, mostly," Alain admitted. "I was trying to make tomatoes that glowed in the dark—don't ask why, it seemed important at the time—and somehow made them drought-resistant instead. Complete failure as a nightlight, but apparently very useful for desert colonies."

This was the man Beth was marrying. Someone who made tomatoes glow because it seemed important at the time. Frankie felt something ease in her chest.

"Distinguished Citizen Blais." The voice cut through the warmth like a scalpel through silk. "How wonderful to see you positively glowing with… anticipation."

First Citizen Celeste Bellemont materialized with the kind of timing that suggested she'd been tracking their movements. The woman who owned half the media networks in Cooperative space could stand in for one of her own presenters. Beautiful, with silver hair sculpted into architectural perfection, clothes that whispered money with every breath, and eyes that catalogued everything like she was already writing headlines.

Beside her stood a younger woman who had to be her

daughter—same cheekbones, same calculating eyes, but softened by youth and what might have been actual kindness.

"First Citizen Bellemont, Vivienne," Beth acknowledged with perfect political warmth. "May I present Citizen Francesca Styles, one of my dearest friends from…" She paused delicately. "From our youth."

"Of course." Celeste's smile could have frozen mercury. "Vivienne, darling, you were asking about Alain's orchid research earlier."

"I was?" Vivienne looked puzzled, then caught her mother's look. "Oh. Yes. The singing flowers."

Alain immediately brightened. "They're just in the temperature-controlled section! The harmonics are best at precisely—"

"Why don't you show her?" Celeste suggested smoothly. "I'm sure Distinguished Blais won't mind sparing you for a moment."

It was masterfully done. Before anyone could object, Alain was leading Vivienne away, already deep in explanation about frequency responses. Vivienne glanced back once, something like apology in her expression.

"Such a brilliant young man," Celeste said. "So focused on his work. One does hope he'll have good guidance in… other areas."

The implication hung in the air like a blade.

But Citizen Bellemont wasn't done. "Tell me, Citizen Styles, do you find it difficult? Returning to a world that's moved on without you?"

Subtle.

Before Frankie could decide that she wasn't going to answer that, the room's energy shifted. Now everyone seemed to have suddenly remembered they were predators pretending to be people. Frankie turned.

David Orr stood in the doorway.

She'd seen him a few years ago, when she'd briefly been on

the family's moon. Her first impression was he was like his father but not quite, a wobbly mirror image.

He wore formal blacks that actually stayed black, with his hair in that ridiculous cyclone style that was apparently fashionable among senators who wanted to seem dynamic. His face was all Konrad—those sharp angles, that mouth that defaulted to disapproval—but softened somehow. Where Konrad was a sword, David was a butter knife that desperately wanted to be more.

"Senator Orr," Beth said, inclining her head precisely the right amount. "How good of you to come."

"Citizen Blais." David's voice had that reedy quality Frankie remembered, at odds with his attempt at gravity. His bushy eyebrows drew together as his gaze found Frankie. "And the cargo pilot. How… unexpectedly delightful."

The cargo pilot. Not Citizen Styles, not even Frankie. The cargo pilot, like she was the help who'd wandered into the wrong room.

"Senator," Frankie said, matching Beth's precise nod. "I'm honored by your welcome."

It was the exact wrong thing to say—too formal, calling attention to his rudeness by being excessively polite. David's face flushed slightly.

"Yes, well." He turned to Morgan, and his expression soured further. "Brother. I see you're wearing… what exactly are you wearing?"

"Fashion," Morgan said cheerfully. "I know you're not familiar with the concept."

"I'm familiar with looking like an adult."

"And I'm familiar with looking like I don't have a small forest creature living on my head, yet here we are."

Beth intervened before the brothers could escalate. "The Regent will be joining us shortly. Perhaps we should take our seats?"

It was phrased as a suggestion but delivered as a command. They dispersed to their assigned places, Frankie finding herself between a minister she vaguely recognized and someone who kept staring at her with the intensity of someone trying to solve a puzzle.

First Citizen Celeste Bellemont.

Fantastic.

Luckily, the poor sod on her left had captured the citizen's attention. Minister of… Agriculture?

The minister beside Frankie—Trade, she remembered from Morgan's briefing—leaned toward her as she sat. "Citizen Styles. Such a pleasure. I haven't seen you since…" She paused delicately. "Well. Since you were much younger."

Since the orphan tour. Since the photos. Since Frankie had been trotted out like a show pony to demonstrate the Cooperative's mercy.

"Yes," Frankie said, unfolding her napkin with practiced ease. "Time does pass."

"Indeed. And now you're a ship captain! How… resourceful of you."

Resourceful. Like work was a hobby Frankie had taken up for fun.

The first course arrived before Frankie could respond to the minister—tiny spheres of pastry that looked like pearls but tasted like the concept of anticipation. The flavor was unsettling, too abstract to be food, too physical to be ignored.

"Molecular gastronomy," the minister said, noticing Frankie's expression. "The chef trained on Praxis. Everything tastes like ideas now."

"How… bold," Frankie managed.

Her hand selected the correct fork without hesitation. Somewhere between the orbital base and the Capital, she'd stopped fighting her training and started using it. The realization should have bothered her more than it did.

The second course was worse—flat discs that dissolved on the tongue and tasted like homesickness. Frankie ate them mechanically, her hand remembering exactly which tiny fork to use, her posture automatically correct.

Morgan, she noticed, was several seats away, trapped between two senators who seemed to be having a competition about who could be more dull. He caught her eye and mimed falling asleep, which earned him a glare from David, farther down the table. Seated next to David, Vivienne Bellemont seemed to be looking past him, watching Alain. Or the empty seat beside him, where the regent should be sitting.

The third course arrived—the first of the fish preparations. Three different types, each requiring different utensils, each with its own specific protocol. Frankie's hand hovered over the array of silver.

Start from the outside. No, that was for Summer service. This was High Galactic formal. The fish fork would be… there. The one that looked like every other fork except for the number of tines and the subtle curve of the handle.

She reached for it just as First Citizen Bellemont finally turned to her.

"I remember. As I was hoping to discuss earlier, you still look just like her."

Frankie's hand froze. "I'm sorry?"

"From the photo. The Child Orphan of Wala." The First's smile was professional, practiced, the kind that appeared above news stories about tragedy. "I ran it on all my networks during the anniversary coverage. Such a powerful image. That poor little girl, realizing she was all alone, forever and ever. My viewers still write in about it."

The fork felt cold in Frankie's hand. "I wouldn't know."

"Even with your hair so short." The First's eyes sharpened with predatory focus. I've wanted to interview you for years. My viewers would be so moved to see how you've… persevered."

Other conversations were stopping. Heads turning. The First's voice carried in that way media voices did when they sensed content.

"Tell me," First Bellemont leaned in, her perfume aggressive with expense, "do you think you could lay hands on the sword? It would be such a powerful visual for the anniversary special I'm planning."

"I—"

"Francesca's work in cargo transport has been fascinating," Beth's voice cut across the table like a scalpel wrapped in silk. "Did you know she's mapped three new trade routes in the Outer Rim? The economic impact has been substantial."

The shift was masterful. Suddenly Frankie wasn't a tragedy to be gawked at but an economic force to be reckoned with. First Citizen Bellemont blinked, thrown off her trajectory.

"Oh. How… industrious."

But the damage was done. Everyone at their end of the table now knew exactly who Frankie was. She could feel their glances like insects on her skin, hear the mental calculations as they tried to reconcile the semi-polished woman in emerald with the grief-stricken child from their history lessons.

Down the table, a voice she didn't recognize: "Of course, Wala chose risky energy mods—everyone knew synth sympathies clouded their judgment."

Frankie's fork paused mid-bite. She forced herself to close her mouth, and swallow etiquette and rage in the same gulp. Neither Wala's energy mods nor its small synthetic human population had anything to do with a random rogue Orr rocket smashing the planet to bits.

The fish course continued, with its interminable protocols.

Frankie ate mechanically, tasting nothing. Her body performed while her mind fled, running down dusty mental corridors, that photo following her like a malevolent ghost.

Then the energy shifted again. Stronger this time. The conversation didn't stop—that would be too obvious—but it stuttered, like everyone had suddenly remembered they might be being graded.

The Regent had arrived.

She entered without fanfare, which was somehow more dramatic than trumpets would have been. Frankie's first thought was that she moved like Beth—that same gliding walk that suggested the floor was honored by her presence. Her second thought was that Beth moved like her.

The Regent was maybe sixty, maybe seventy—the kind of age that had stopped mattering because she'd decided it didn't. Her face was a masterwork of preservation, not young but somehow timeless. Beautiful in the way mountains were beautiful, shaped by pressure and time into something that could weather anything.

She wore midnight blue so dark it was almost black, with jewelry that managed to be both subtle and worth more than the Spear. Her hair was silver, styled in a complex arrangement that looked effortless and probably took three hours to achieve.

But it was her presence that filled the room. Beth had presence —Frankie had felt it earlier, that ability to reshape space around herself. But if Beth was a sun, the Regent was a black hole. Everything bent toward her, even light.

Dame Celeste's spine straightened imperceptibly, and she glanced at her daughter, who matched her rigid posture.

The Regent took her seat at the head of the table without acknowledging anyone specific, but somehow everyone felt acknowledged. Or assessed. Or both.

"Continue," she said, and her voice was Beth's voice aged in oak barrels. Warm on the surface, with depths that could drown you.

Conversation resumed, but carefully now. The fourth course arrived—something meaty that looked like architecture and tasted like ambition. Frankie ate it without registering more than texture.

The Regent's gaze moved around the table like a searchlight. When it reached Frankie, it stopped.

"Citizen Styles."

Two words, but they carried the weight of years. Of decisions made in committee rooms. Of a signature on papers that made Frankie a ward of the state. Of every formal dinner where a terrified child had sat at tables like this and tried not to cry.

"My regent," Frankie managed, doing that odd bend-forward move that stood in for a bow when one was seated.

"I'm pleased you could join us." The words were warm. The delivery was assessment. "Beth speaks highly of your work in the Outer Rim."

"The Outer Rim has been… educational."

"I imagine so." The Regent's smile was a masterpiece— genuine warmth layered over political calculation layered over something else Frankie couldn't read. "Distance often provides perspective."

There were seventeen different ways to interpret that. Frankie chose the safest. "It's been valuable to see how different systems approach common problems."

"Yes. Different approaches." The Regent's gaze hadn't moved. "Though some problems remain remarkably consistent, don't they? No matter where we go."

Everyone was listening now, even while pretending they weren't. This was what they'd come for—to watch the Regent work, to parse meanings from meanings, to see if the target of her interest would crumble.

"Consistency can be instructive," Frankie said carefully. "Patterns teach us what's fundamental versus what's merely habitual."

Something shifted in the Regent's expression. Approval? Surprise? "Indeed. Though habits, I find, are often more honest than principles."

"Perhaps. But principles are more photogenic."

The words were out before Frankie could stop them. The reference to the photo, to principles versus reality, to the whole performance of mercy that had shaped her life.

The table held its breath.

The Regent smiled. A real smile this time, sharp as winter. "Yes. They certainly are."

She turned her attention elsewhere, releasing Frankie like a cat releasing a mouse it had decided wasn't worth eating. Yet.

The rest of the dinner passed in a blur of courses that tasted like concepts and conversations that meant nothing. Morgan delighted his dull seatmates, or at least got them to smile. The contrast with his brother was stunning, even if she couldn't hear their words.

David tried to make cutting remarks, judging by his expression, but his small audience just looked confused. He had his father's face but not his father's instinct for the jugular.

Morgan's outfit, however, seemed to take personal offense at David's attempts. During the sixth course—something that resembled a spiderweb and tasted like regret—his jacket suddenly froze mid-shift between colors, half midnight black, half electric blue. The fabric seized up with an audible electrical buzz that drew every eye at their end of the table.

"New fashion statement?" David asked with a smirk.

"Just giving everyone something interesting to look at," Morgan replied smoothly, though Frankie caught the flash of panic in his eyes. He tapped discreetly at his collar, which only made the situation worse—the blue portion began to pulse rhythmically, like a techno heartbeat.

A nearby senator leaned in, fascinated. "Is it meant to do that?"

"Absolutely," Morgan assured her with complete confidence. "It's responding to the dinner conversation. Blue pulses indicate pretentiousness levels have exceeded safety protocols."

The senator blinked, then burst into unexpected laughter. Three other guests immediately began asking where they might acquire similar attire, while David seethed silently.

By the dessert course, Morgan had somehow transformed the malfunction into the evening's most coveted fashion innovation.

Finally, after what felt like several decades, the Regent rose. Everyone else scrambled to stand, napkins clutched, conversations dying mid-syllable.

"A lovely evening," she said to the room. To Beth. To the air. "I look forward to celebrating with you all at tomorrow's garden party."

She left, taking the room's center of gravity with her. People began to disperse, carefully casual, nobody wanting to seem too eager to escape.

"Well," Morgan said, appearing at Frankie's elbow. "That was bracing. I particularly enjoyed the part where Celeste Bellemont tried to collect you like a trading card."

"I liked when your brother called me 'the cargo pilot' like it was a disease."

"Classic David. He's practiced that sneer in the mirror for years. Never quite gets it right." Morgan's outfit had given up on subtlety and was now cycling through colors like an anxious rainbow. "Ready to escape?"

"Beyond ready."

They made their goodbyes—Beth hugged her with real warmth but political timing, Alain invited her to see his singing orchids properly, David ignored them entirely. The walk back to the suite felt like swimming up from deep water.

In the hallway, finally away from performed conversations and edible concepts, Frankie could breathe again. The jeweled dress felt heavier now, like it had absorbed the weight of everyone's stares.

"For what it's worth," Morgan said as his outfit finally admitted defeat and turned a normal black, "you handled that brilliantly."

"I ate food that tasted like regret and let someone ask me about the worst day of my life."

"Yes, but you did it with excellent posture."

Despite everything, Frankie laughed. It came out shaky, but it was real. "Is that what matters?"

"Here? Unfortunately." He paused at her door. "Oh, before I forget. I got an invitation to tomorrow's garden party."

Relief flooded through her. At least she wouldn't have to face it alone. "Good. We can—"

"As Celine's plus-one."

The relief curdled. "Oh."

"Yeah." Morgan's expression was complicated. "Apparently she's invited to the wedding.."

Celine. The gorgeous, brilliant woman who Morgan's family wanted him to marry. Who belonged in this world in all the ways Frankie didn't.

"That's… that'll be nice for you."

"Nice. Right." He shifted, uncomfortable. "You'll be fine. It's a garden party, much less formal. And Spike will probably wake up by then."

"Spike!" Frankie had completely forgotten.

She opened the door to find the cyvlossic exactly where they'd left her, sprawled on the loveseat in a puddle of afternoon sun that had long since moved on. She was snoring.

Only, something was different. Frankie blinked. Spike's fur gleamed with an unnatural perfection—each tuft meticulously shaped, her gray and black markings somehow more defined. There was a faint scent of something expensive in the air, like cedar and citrus.

"Did she even notice we were gone?" Morgan asked.

Frankie stepped closer to inspect the transformation. Spike opened one eye, yawned magnificently to display unusually white teeth, then closed it again. The eye had opened just long enough for Frankie to catch a hint of something smug in it.

Frankie noticed a folded note on the side table. She picked it up.

Citizen Styles,

The Zichi Cyvlossic Spa & Grooming Center was delighted to host your companion this evening. The first session is complimentary for distinguished guests, but we must respectfully request that visits be scheduled in advance through proper channels hereafter. Please find attached the services provided, for your records.

Regards,

Proctor Venn, Guest Services

Frankie unfolded the itemized list and choked on a laugh.

**Premium Coat Revitalization*

**Claw Buffing & Shaping*

**Ear Tuft Sculpting (Extra Volume)*

**Dental Brightening*

**Complimentary Organic Treats (7 consumed)*

"You snuck out to the spa?" Frankie couldn't decide whether to be impressed or concerned. "How did you even find it?"

Spike stretched languidly, showing off her immaculate coat, and gave Frankie a look that clearly said: *I have my ways.*

Frankie looked up at Morgan. "I didn't bring her anything. I meant to, but after the photo thing—"

"Already handled." Morgan produced a small wrapped

package from one of his impossible pockets. "Real food. Not concepts. Not ideas. Actual protein that tastes like protein."

The package was surprisingly large for something that had fit in his pocket. It was wrapped in what appeared to be formal dinner napkins.

"How did you—"

"I charmed one of the servers. Told them it was for a sick relative. Which isn't entirely false—Spike is probably sick of kibble." He patted his jacket, which rustled suspiciously. "These dimensional pockets come in handy when dinner tastes like existential dread instead of calories."

He leaned in conspiratorially. "I've been smuggling real food out of these events for months. There's an entire shadow economy among the staff—they save the actual ingredients for people who want sustenance instead of art." He pulled another wrapped something out.

"There's a sandwich in there that tastes exactly like a sandwich. Revolutionary concept, I know. And some pastry that I'm told has actual sugar, not distilled happiness or whatever they were serving for dessert."

Frankie took the package, something easing in her chest. "Thank you."

"Partners in crime, remember?" He gave a crooked smile. "Get some rest. Tomorrow's the garden party, and if tonight was any indication, it's going to be… interesting."

He left, and Frankie closed the door on the hallway, the Complex, the whole performed world. She set the package of real food next to Spike, who cracked an eye open and made a sound that might have been approval.

"You had the right idea," Frankie told her, starting the complex process of escaping the jeweled dress. "Sleep through the whole thing."

Tomorrow was the garden party. More politics, more performances, more chances for someone to ask about that photo. But at least there would be real flowers instead of singing ones. And Morgan would be there, even if he was with Celine.

She'd survived one formal dinner. She could survive a garden party.

Probably.

The dress finally released her, and Frankie breathed properly for the first time in hours. She looked down at herself and winced. The bodice had left a lattice of red indentations across her ribs, like a map of trade routes pressed into her skin. The jeweled embellishments had branded tiny hexagonal patterns into her shoulders.

"Fashion battle scars," she muttered, rubbing at a particularly vivid mark.

She tried to drape the dress over a chair, but it slithered to the floor with alarming sentience. When she attempted to hang it in the closet, it somehow became entangled with three other garments, as if refusing to be contained. After the third attempt, she gave up and left it draped half on, half off a chair, where it pooled like expensive resentment.

Tomorrow she'd have to do it all again. But tonight, she had a freshly-groomed snoring cyvlossic, food that would taste like food, and a door between her and the rest of the Complex.

Couldn't get better than that.

CHAPTER
SEVEN

FRANKIE'S DOOR chimed at 0730 exactly. Of course Beth would still be punctual to the second.

"I brought breakfast," she announced, sweeping in with a covered tray before Frankie could properly respond. She wore the daily uniform of a Distinguished Citizen—today in blue and cream, perfectly pressed—but her hair was in the simple braid they'd worn as girls, not the elaborate style from last night.

"Real coffee," Beth continued, setting the tray on the low table. "And those terrible protein biscuits you used to love. The kitchen still had the recipe filed under 'Francesca-breakfast-standard.'" She grinned. "I may have threatened the morning cook with bureaucratic paperwork if he tried to 'improve' them."

"My hero," Frankie said, sinking onto the cushion across from Beth. Without thinking, she tucked her left leg under—Academy breakfast posture.

Beth noticed and deliberately mirrored the position. "Some things are worth keeping," she said softly.

They uncovered the tray together, revealing not just the promised biscuits and coffee, but also fresh fruit arranged in an old pattern—a lopsided face that had once made Proctor Lizbet purse her lips in disapproval.

"Oh, you didn't," Frankie laughed.

"I absolutely did. Made it myself while the cook had his back turned." Beth's eyes sparkled with mischief. "He nearly fainted when he saw the Distinguished Citizen-Presumptive 'defacing' the breakfast presentation."

For a few minutes, they just ate and talked—Beth catching her up on Complex gossip, Frankie sharing sanitized trader stories. It felt like being kids again, stealing moments between lessons.

"I know I was stressed last night," Beth said eventually, cradling her coffee cup. "That weird accident has everyone on edge. Lucien's security team wants him to skip the ceremony entirely."

"But?"

"But the Regent told them that's ridiculous. We can't live in fear." Beth's jaw set in a familiar stubborn line. "Besides, I have you here now. Remember when we figured out who was stealing from the kitchens? You saw the pattern in the delivery schedules before anyone else."

"That was just logic—"

"That was brilliance, and you know it." Beth leaned forward. "I've gotten better at seeing patterns too. Comes with the job. But I missed having someone to puzzle things out with. The Regent's advisors all have agendas. Alain can't be bothered, unless it's plant related. You're the only person who ever just helped me think."

Frankie felt her throat tighten. "Beth—"

"I'm not asking you to stay," Beth said quickly. "I know your life is out there. But great Safra, Frankie, I'm glad you're here now. Even if it's just for a few days." She paused, then added with determined cheer, "Besides, someone needs to keep Morgan from wearing anything too disastrous to the wedding."

"His outfit last night defied several laws of physics."

"And taste. And possibly nature itself." Beth giggled, then sobered. "How is he doing? Really? I know Celine has been… distant."

"He's figuring it out. Growing up, maybe?"

"Aren't we all." Beth reached across the table and squeezed Frankie's hand. "I know things are different now. I'm marrying into a great family, you're trading across the galaxy, we can't have breakfast every morning anymore. But Frankie—you're still my best friend. That doesn't change just because everything else does."

Frankie squeezed back. "Still best friends. Even when you're the Distinguished Citizen and I'm just a smuggler in a snowman ship."

"Alleged smuggler," Beth corrected primly, then grinned.

They dissolved into laughter, and for a moment they were just Beth and Frankie again, best friends figuring out the world together.

"I should go," Beth said eventually, but she was smiling. "Morning briefing. But dinner tomorrow? Just us and Morgan and Spike? I'll have food sent to your quarters. We can eat like normal people."

"I'd love that."

At the door, Beth turned back. "Oh, and Frankie? When this is all over—the wedding, the ceremony, the politics—I want to hear everything. Every adventure, every close call, every ridiculous thing Spike has done. Promise?"

"Promise."

FRANKIE SAT on the edge of one of the sofas in her suite, her bare feet oddly light without the familiar weight of gravity boots.

She'd changed into her second-best tunic, a soft blue that wasn't trying too hard, and comfortable pants that everyone the Complex would probably faint if they saw.

But this wasn't for the Complex. This was for Elin and Sigrid. Ellen and Joy, she corrected herself. The names they'd chosen, the lives they'd built.

Spike finished her own lunch—the last of the real food Morgan had smuggled from dinner—and padded over to flop across Frankie's feet. The weight was grounding, familiar. Unlike everything else in this place.

The suite's holo-display flickered to life, hovering over the coffee table, but Frankie had set it to flat view. No need for three-dimensional projections that would make the distance between them feel like judgment. The purple-gold seal of Beth's priority clearance spiraled across the screen. These calls would cost more than a month of fuel, but Beth had insisted. "Use it for anything you need," she'd said. "Anything that helps."

As if anything could help.

The first connection went through quickly. Ellen—Elin, her mind still insisted—appeared on the screen, and Frankie's chest tightened with a mix of joy and loss.

She looked good. Older, obviously, but good. Her dark hair was shorter now, practical, pulled back in a clip that was purely functional. Her face had new lines, the kind that came from squinting at screens all day, calculating critical equations. She wore standard-issue terraforming crew clothes, gray-green and designed to be forgotten.

Behind her was nothing. A blank gray wall in what was obviously a communication booth. The kind every long-term base had, where crew could call home without anyone overhearing their homesickness.

"Freddie," Ellen said, using her old nickname. Ellen's voice was exactly the same: quiet, measured, with those pauses that made you suspect she was thinking three steps ahead. Her eyes, though—her eyes kept moving, flicking to corners of the blank booth like she was reading invisible data.

"Ellen." Frankie managed a smile. "You look well."

"You look…" Ellen's gaze settled on her for a moment, actually seeing. "Happy. Despite being back there."

"It's temporary. Just for the wedding."

"Ah." Ellen's eyes resumed their restless scanning. "Beth's transformation of grief into celebration. Very her."

"You got the invitation?"

"I got several. Email, official post, even a personal note on real paper." A ghost of a smile. "She was always thorough."

"But you're not coming."

"Freddie." Ellen leaned back slightly, the booth's harsh lighting throwing shadows under her eyes. "I'm seventeen light-years away, currently trying to save forty thousand colonists whose atmospheric processors are failing. Even if I could leave— which I can't—it would take me eight weeks to get there."

"I know. I just… I hoped."

"You hoped for a miracle." Ellen's voice was gentle but firm. "We stopped believing in those twenty-five years ago."

Silence stretched between them, filled with everything they weren't saying. Spike adjusted on Frankie's feet, a warm reminder of the present.

"Tell me about your work," Frankie said finally. "The colonists."

Ellen's whole demeanor shifted, animation flickering into her expression. "It's a mess. Previous terraforming team cut corners, used sub-standard processors. We're having to rebuild the entire atmospheric conversion system while people are still breathing. It's…" She paused, searching for words. "It's the kind of puzzle that matters."

"Saving forty thousand people."

"Giving them a future." Ellen's eyes finally stilled, focusing on something beyond the screen. "A real one. Not borrowed time on a dead world."

Like Wala, Frankie thought but didn't say. Their beautiful, stubborn planet that had refused Cooperative membership, insisted on independence, and paid the ultimate price.

"Do you ever think about it?" Frankie asked softly. "The anniversary?"

Ellen blinked. "What anniversary?"

"When Wala—"

"Oh." Ellen's expression went carefully blank. "I don't really track dates anymore. Base time, planetary rotations, it all blurs together. Easier that way."

She didn't remember. Or had trained herself not to. Frankie felt something twist in her chest.

"Besides," Ellen continued, her voice taking on that practical tone Frankie remembered from childhood, "dwelling on the past doesn't help anyone. Not the colonists here, not the planets I'll terraform next, not..." She paused. "Not us."

"The memorial Beth designed is beautiful," Frankie offered. "If you wanted to see—"

"No." The word was sharp, immediate. Then softer: "No, thank you. I've moved forward, Freddie. This is my life now. Making worlds livable. Giving people homes they won't lose."

"I understand."

"Do you?" Ellen leaned forward slightly. "You're still there. Still in the Capital, wearing their clothes, speaking their language, playing their games. You and Beth both."

"I left. I'm a cargo pilot now, I live on the edges—"

"But you returned." Ellen's eyes resumed their restless motion. "You always return."

Frankie didn't have an answer for that.

"I should go," Ellen said after a moment. "Shift change coming up, and someone else needs the booth."

"Ellen—Elin—"

"It's Ellen." For the first time, real emotion flickered across her face. "Elin was a scared little girl who watched her world burn. Ellen builds new ones. I like Ellen better."

"I love you," Frankie said quietly. "Both versions."

Something softened in Ellen's expression. "I know. But Freddie… let her go. Let them all go. The dead don't need our tears anymore."

The connection ended, leaving Frankie staring at her own reflection in the dark screen. Spike made a questioning noise, and Frankie reached down to scratch behind her ears.

"One down," she murmured. "One to go."

And that was the easy one.

She stood, needing to move, to shake off Ellen's carefully constructed distance. Her feet felt strange against the carpet. She paced to the molecular gastronomy unit, its tiers of gleaming equipment promising drinks that would taste like feelings.

No. The last thing she needed was a beverage that might taste like abandonment or survivor's guilt or whatever emotion the machine decided she wanted to have.

She paced back to the loveseat and sat, jamming her feet under Spike's warm weight. The cyvlossic grumbled but adjusted, sprawling more heavily across Frankie's ankles. Better. Anchored.

The second call took longer to connect. Joy—Sigrid, her heart insisted—lived closer to the Capital but somehow felt further away. When the screen finally lit up, Frankie couldn't help but smile.

Joy was surrounded by chaos. Behind her, a den straight out of a family holo-drama—books scattered on every surface, a picture window showing rolling hills and what might be vineyards, the sound of children thundering past. Joy herself looked… fulfilled. That was the word. Her round face had laugh lines, her hair was in a messy bun that spoke of a morning spent wrangling kids, and she wore a tunic with what appeared to be grape juice stains.

"Freddie!" Joy's voice was warm but wary. "I almost didn't pick up when I saw that purple monstrosity of a seal. Thought it might be Beth herself calling."

"Just me. Using her clearance, though."

"Of course you are." Joy turned away from the screen. "Kids! OUT! Mama's on an important call!" The thundering increased, punctuated by giggles. A door slammed. Joy turned back, grinning. "Sorry. Afternoon energy surge. All ten of them get it at the same time."

"Ten?"

"We adopt the hard-to-place ones," Joy said with pride. "The older kids, the ones with trauma, the ones who've been passed around. Ketch and I figured we knew something about starting over."

Ketch—her husband. Frankie had looked him up once. A vintner from an old family, nothing to do with politics or the Capital or any of it. He'd fallen in love with Sigrid-who-became-Joy and never asked about the before times.

"That's wonderful," Frankie said, meaning it.

"It's chaos." Joy settled back into what was clearly her favorite chair, worn leather that had molded to her shape. "Beautiful, exhausting chaos. So different from…" She paused, studying Frankie through the screen. "So how's that going over?"

"The hair?" Frankie touched her hair self-consciously. "It's been interesting. Someone mistook me for service staff."

Joy laughed, sharp and knowing. "Of course they did. Capital never changes. Still the same poisonous performance, just new costumes." Her expression hardened. "Which is why I'm not coming to the wedding."

"Joy—"

"No, Freddie. Don't." Joy leaned forward, intensity replacing warmth. "Do you know what Beth's doing? Using that date? It's obscene."

"She thinks it's healing—"

"It's erasure." Joy's voice cracked like a whip. "She's taking the worst day of our lives and putting ribbons on it. Making it about her happiness instead of our loss."

"She lost everything, too—"

"Did she?" Joy stood abruptly, pacing in front of the screen. Her camera was slow to catch up, giving Frankie a view of her waist. And her fisted hands. "Beth thrived there. Loved every minute of the apology tour, the attention, the chance to be special. While we were dying inside, she was planning her political career."

"That's not fair."

"Isn't it?" Joy stopped pacing, fixing Frankie with a look that cut deep. "You and Beth, you were so lucky. The sword changed everything for you."

The sword. Frankie's hand moved unconsciously to her throat.

"We all survived because of that sword," she said quietly.

"You survived as celebrities. Ellen and I survived as refugees." Joy's voice carried old bitterness. "Do you know why we were both adopted so quickly? Why you and Beth weren't even given that option?"

Frankie shook her head, though she'd suspected.

"They wanted you. The Cooperative, the media, the whole machine. The two photogenic orphans who'd discovered proof of ancient civilizations, who'd been special enough to be invited off-planet before disaster struck. Ellen and I were afterthoughts. Boring, forgettable afterthoughts."

"We didn't ask for—"

"I know." Joy sank back into her chair, the fight leaving her as quickly as it had come. "I know you didn't. But you kept it. Both of you. Beth turned it into power, and you… you're still carrying it around like armor that doesn't fit."

They sat in silence for a moment. One of Joy's kids peeked around the door, was shooed away with a gentle hand gesture.

"Where's that sword anyway?" Joy asked suddenly. "Still at the University?"

"I… I don't know. I haven't thought about it in years."

"You should find out." Joy's expression was unreadable. "You and Beth, always together. Always a team. And you still are."

"We're different—"

"Are you?" Joy gestured at the screen. "You're there. Using her clearance, attending her wedding, playing dress-up in the Capital. You've stayed too long in that life to ever get away from it now."

"I did get away. I'm a pilot, I live on the edges—"

"But you go back." Joy's voice was gentle now, sad. "Best you can do is keep that physical distance. You do look happier now, Freddie. Hold onto that. As for Beth…" She shrugged. "If she thinks she can do some good in that nest of vipers, more power to her. But she's swimming in poison and calling it wine."

"She's trying to change things."

"From inside the belly of the beast? Good luck with that." Joy glanced off-screen, listening to something. "I need to go. Evening feeding soon, and if I'm not there, they'll have Ketch convinced they need dessert first."

Frankie wasn't getting through. "Sigrid—"

"It's Joy. Joy Ketchill. Mother of ten, maker of adequate wine, keeper of chaos." She smiled, and for a moment Frankie saw the girl she'd been. "That other name belongs to a dead girl on a dead planet. Let her rest."

"Someone brought up the photo at dinner last night," Frankie said quickly, before Joy could disconnect. "The famous one."

Joy's face went still. "Of course they did. Your tragedy, their entertainment. Did you tell them where they could shove their sympathy?"

"Beth intervened."

"Of course she did. Can't have scandal at a formal dinner." Joy shook her head. "This is why I stay away, Freddie. This is why we all should stay away."

"I love you," Frankie said, echoing what she'd told Ellen. "All of you. However you've survived."

Joy's expression softened one last time. "I know. But love doesn't mean we have to relive the terrible times just because Beth wants to play bride on its anniversary." She paused. "Be careful, Freddie. The Capital takes more than it gives. Always has."

The screen went dark.

Frankie sat in the perfect silence of the suite, her feet numb under Spike's weight. Two calls. Two rejections. Two completely different women who'd once been girls she'd shared everything with.

Ellen, who'd forgotten the date and built new worlds.

Joy, who remembered everything and protected her new family from it.

And somewhere in this perfect, poisonous Complex, Beth was planning to transform their shared trauma into flower arrangements and formal vows.

Spike shifted, looking up at her with those unsettling eyes.

"They're right, aren't they?" Frankie said softly. "I do keep coming back. Like a moth to a flame that already burned me once."

Spike's response was to knead her claws into Frankie's foot, just hard enough to hurt.

"Ow. Okay, okay. Existential crisis later." She checked the time. Two hours until the garden party. Two hours to transform back into Citizen Styles, grateful orphan, Beth's oldest friend.

Well, at least she wouldn't have to manage Ellen and Joy through it all. The thought brought a wave of relief so strong it made her dizzy. She loved them, missed them, wanted them in her life—but not here. Not performing grief and gratitude for people who saw their tragedy as heartwarming backstory.

They'd chosen their paths. Ellen fixing worlds, Joy raising children, both of them free.

And Frankie? Still caught between the cargo pilot she'd become and the orphan she'd been. Still coming back when Beth called. Still playing dress-up in a world that didn't fit.

But that was her choice, wasn't it? Her path. Messy and complicated and probably unhealthy, but hers.

"Come on," she said to Spike, gently extracting her feet. "Let's find something garden-party appropriate. Something that says 'I'm just here for the flowers' instead of 'please ask me about my tragic past.' Or my plushie-plush cyvlossic."

Spike yawned and padded toward the bedroom.

CHAPTER
EIGHT

THE REGENT'S garden bloomed under glass, a terrarium for people who thought nature needed improvement.

Frankie paused at the entrance arch—living vines trained into submission—and let her eyes adjust to the golden afternoon light. The dome above created its own weather: perfect temperature, perfect humidity that was just a touch too high, perfect condensation beading on the glass walls like the space was sweating from the effort of being ideal.

Spike pressed warm against her thigh, ears forward, alert. In front of them, the garden sprawled in calculated wilderness. Paths that seemed to wander actually led visitors through specific sight lines. Flower beds that appeared random followed mathematical principles of color theory. Even the "wild" corner, where native plants were allowed to mingle, had been carefully curated for maximum "authenticity."

White faux-wood tables dotted the open central green like mushrooms after rain, each with four matching chairs that someone had decided needed chartreuse cushions.

"Citizen Styles, how wonderful that you could—" Beth's voice carried that political warmth, the kind that welcomed everyone and no one. She stood just inside the entrance, positioned to greet each arrival with maximum efficiency. Then she actually looked at who she was greeting. "Frankie!"

The transformation was instant. Political Beth melted away, replaced by actual Beth—tired Beth, happy Beth, slightly frustrated Beth.

"Oh thank Saf—the gods," she said, pulling Frankie into a quick, real hug that smelled of jasmine and exhaustion. "I thought this was going to be an afternoon for us. Tea and terrible jokes about the wedding planning and—" She gestured at the carefully dressed crowds already mingling among the flora. "But the Regent insisted. 'Informal preview for key families.'" Her voice took on the Regent's measured tones. "As if anything here is ever informal."

"Beth—"

"No, it's fine. It's good practice." The mask started sliding back into place as new guests appeared behind Frankie. "Alain's around somewhere, probably explaining root systems to someone who just wanted cucumber sandwiches. Save me a real conversation for later?"

"Of course."

"Wonderful." Full Political Beth returned as she looked past Frankie. "Minister Chen-Okoye! How delightful that you could join us..."

Frankie moved deeper into the garden, Spike still velcroed to her side. The paths were wide enough for proper mingling but narrow enough to force conversations. Already she could see the afternoon's choreography: groups forming and reforming, political affiliation displayed through proximity, careful distances maintained between rivals.

And everywhere, cyvlossics.

The ultimate accessory. Rare, gorgeous—most of them—and

devoted to their one person. There was Sterling, Senator Voss's silver-gray shadow, sitting at perfect attention beside the refreshment pavilion. Prism, with her color-shifting coat, giving notice that her person, First Citizen Celeste Bellemont, was on the prowl. And now Honey, Minister Chen-Okoye's golden-haired beauty.

Watching them all, Spike's head tilted, confused. Frankie could see it, too. Why did the cyvlossics keep looking at each other? Quick glances across the garden, silent communication that their owners didn't notice.

"Frankie!" Morgan's voice saved her from analyzing further. He stood near a tortuous vertical orchid display that probably cost more than fuel for a jump. Celine stood beside him, smiling tall, blond, in a dress that managed to be both casual and perfectly tailored. "Come see Alain's new hybrids. They smell like cinnamon, but only on Tuesdays."

Frankie made her way over, footsteps soft on the mossy grass, noting how Morgan looked actually relaxed. His outfit had given up on color-changing drama and settled on a deep green that complemented the garden. Celine's hand rested lightly on his arm.

"That can't be true," Celine was saying, looking at the droopy flowers. "Plants don't know what day it is."

"They do if you program their circadian rhythms to a seven-day cycle," Morgan said. "Alain thought it would be romantic. The wedding's on a Tuesday, so—"

"So the whole place will smell like cinnamon." Celine shook her head, but she was smiling. Smile dimming, she looked at Frankie. "Your almost-brother-in-law is deeply weird," she said.

"The best kind of weird," Frankie said

Celine's gaze turned cool, assessing. "Frankie. You look well. The Capital suits you."

It was so perfectly wrong that Frankie almost laughed. "Like a suit made of knives, maybe."

"The best armor often is," Celine said. "I'm sorry we didn't get to spend more time together when you were on Cloud. But I suspect your departure was perfectly timed."

Celine would know. She had given her off-moon transit ticket to Frankie at the last minute, when a rescue Frankie was trying to accomplish almost went off the rails. Celine had spent the evening with Morgan instead, and that had worked out nicely for all of them.

Morgan winced. "About that—"

"Citizen Styles!" Minister Chen-Okoye appeared at Frankie's elbow with almost too much energy. She was handsome in the way powerful people often were, with silver threading through her jet-black hair and accessories that whispered rather than shouted their worth. "I've been hoping to meet you properly. Your work in establishing the Outer Rim routes has been a boon for our agricultural exports."

"Minister." Frankie inclined her head properly, muscle memory kicking in.

"Please, call me Adaeze. We're all informal here." She laughed at her own joke. "I wanted to thank you particularly for the Harvest Station route. We've been able to ship preservation-resistant crops for the first time in decades."

Behind the minister, Honey sat like a golden shadow. The cyvlossic was beautiful in the way all of them were—too perfect to be natural, too alive to be artificial. Her coat gleamed like actual honey in sunlight, and her eyes held that unsettling intelligence all cyvlossics shared.

But something was off. Instead of maintaining the proper distance behind her owner, Honey pressed forward, actually brushing against the Minister's legs. And she kept looking at the other cyvlossics.

"Honey, darling, what's gotten into you?" Adaeze reached down absently to pet her companion. "She's been like this all day. Desperate for attention."

"She's always been affectionate," Morgan said, and something in his voice made Frankie look at him sharply. "Even as a kitten. That's why I named her Honey—sweet as honey, always wanting cuddles."

Celine laughed, a gentle bell. "That's right. You named all of them."

"They needed names." Morgan said it casually, but Frankie caught the flicker of something—regret? nostalgia?—in his expression. "Sterling was this serious little gray kit who sat at attention even while playing. Jade would disappear into shadows until you forgot she was there. Prism's coat started changing colors the day she opened her eyes."

"That's…" Celine paused, visibly recalibrating. "Actually quite sweet."

Honey, apparently deciding Morgan's reminiscence was an invitation, abandoned her owner entirely and wound around his legs like a furry golden river. Morgan laughed, dropping to one knee to give her proper attention.

"Hello, beautiful," he murmured, hands finding a spot behind her ears that made her purr. "Been a long time, hasn't it? You've filled out nicely. Getting enough treats from your minister?"

Honey's purr could have powered a small engine. She pressed her head into his hands, whole body vibrating with contentment.

Spike made a sound like someone had insulted her ancestors.

Frankie glanced down at her companion. Every line of Spike's body radiated disdain.

"Problem?" Frankie murmured.

Spike's response was to turn her back on the entire scene and stalk away, tail bristling with offended dignity.

"Well," Morgan said, still petting Honey, "someone's not a fan of public displays of affection."

"Spike's not a fan of public displays of anything," Frankie said, watching her companion disappear behind a cluster of flowering shrubs. She'd probably go find somewhere to sulk. Or shed on something expensive.

"Your companion is quite striking," Minister Chen-Okoye said, though her tone suggested 'striking' wasn't entirely a compliment. "Such unusual coloring."

"She's an original," Frankie agreed.

The conversation meandered through safe topics—trade routes, agricultural yields, the wedding preparations. Morgan kept one hand on Honey, who had achieved a state of bliss usually reserved for religious experiences. Celine contributed quite a bit, her knowledge of interplanetary commerce surprisingly deep. Minister Chen-Okoye probed gently for information about Frankie's routes, clearly hoping for advantage.

Normal garden party stuff, except for the way other cyvlossics kept glancing their way. Sterling, still at his post by the refreshments, watched Honey's display with something like longing. A dark-coated cyvlossic Frankie didn't recognize tracked their group with green eyes that caught the light.

"Oh!" Alain's voice preceded him through a hedge of white roses. "You found the orchids! Did you smell them? Well, you wouldn't yet, it's Sunday. But on Tuesday—"

He emerged with leaves in his hair and dirt on his formal yellow-gold tunic, Beth trailing behind him with the expression of someone who'd rounded him up before.

"Alain was showing Senator Voss's aide the root systems," she said dryly. "With visual demonstrations."

"They wanted to know about the filtration applications!" Alain protested. "You can't explain mycorrhizal networks without showing the fungal threads."

"You can when the demonstration involves digging up the heritage roses."

"I'll replant them. They're very forgiving. Unlike the Twilight ferns, which hold grudges." He noticed their blank stares. "That's a joke. Mostly. The ferns do seem to remember environmental stresses and adjust their growth accordingly, which could be interpreted as—"

"Darling." Beth's voice held fond exasperation. "The Minister was discussing trade routes."

"Oh! Yes. Very important. Food security depends on reliable transport." Alain's face brightened. "Francesca, did you know your route modifications reduced spoilage by fifteen percent? I've been able to ship strains that were previously too delicate for long-distance transport."

The conversation fractured and reformed. Alain drew Morgan and the minister into a discussion about preservation techniques. Beth commanded Celine's attention with questions about her family's business. Frankie found herself momentarily alone, free to observe.

David Orr stood at the edge of the Voss contingent, and everything about his position was wrong. Not part of the group but not separate. Close enough to hear their conversation but angled away, like a planet in an unstable orbit. Senator Voss—slate-gray hair, military bearing, the kind of woman who'd eaten bigger fish than David for breakfast—seemed to be pretending he wasn't there.

Sterling, still at perfect attention, kept glancing between David and his owner. Each time David failed to acknowledge him, the silver cyvlossic's ears twitched. Just slightly.

"Fascinating, isn't it?" Celeste Bellemont materialized at Frankie's elbow. "The garden party dynamics. Better than any drama my networks produce."

Today the media magnate wore flowing silver that complemented her hair. Her smile was professional, but her eyes were recording everything. Maybe literally, even though this was officially a no-recording zone.

"First Citizen Bellemont." Frankie managed not to step back.

"Please, after our conversation last night, you must call me Celeste." The smile sharpened. "I've been hoping to continue our discussion about your remarkable journey. My viewers adore a redemption narrative: poor girl from a reckless planet learns manners!"

Frankie ground her molars into a closed-lip smile. Behind Celeste, a cyvlossic padded into view—Prism. The creature's coat really was extraordinary, shifting through colors like oil on water. Currently, she seemed to be cycling through anxious purples and greens.

"I'm afraid there's not much more to tell," Frankie said.

"Oh, I doubt that. A woman who goes from orphan to frontier mapmaker? There's always more to tell." Celeste's gaze flicked to where Spike had disappeared. "Your companion, for instance. Such an unusual choice. Most people prefer their animals more… polished."

"Spike's perfect as she is."

"Of course. Character over beauty. How refreshing." Celeste gestured to where Morgan was still engaged with Alain's impromptu botany lecture. "Young Citizen Orr seems quite taken with your friend Beth's fiancé."

"They share interests."

"Mm. And his companion—Celine Brtzo, isn't it? Lovely girl. Her family's queuing up for mineral rights in the Outer Rim." The observation dangled like bait. "Perhaps you know their operations?"

Frankie was saved from responding by a commotion in the wild corner of the garden. Not loud—cyvlossics were never loud —but a ripple of movement that drew attention.

All the cyvlossics were leaving, headed toward the bushes and the wild area. Sterling had abandoned his post. Honey had left Morgan's side, but not without a sad glance back at him. Even the shadow-dark one Frankie had noticed earlier, was on the move.

And in the lead, just visible through the carefully wild foliage, was Spike.

"Odd," Celeste said. "I've never seen them wander off like that."

And they shouldn't be. Cyvlossics stayed with their owners, maintained proper distances, performed their roles as perfect companions. They didn't go on what looked like a team safari in the middle of of a garden party.

"If you'll excuse me," Frankie said, already moving. Following the furry crowd.

She wound through the garden paths, slipping past a junior minister who took too long to get his question out and a socialite who'd "just loved that old photo" of her.

Just inside the deeper shadow of the tall hedge that divided tame from wild, she saw them.

CHAPTER
NINE

IN THE SHADE OF THE 'WILD' part of the Regent's garden, among the white birches and red cedars, the afternoon air carried the buzz of busy insects and the scent of loam. At the deepest point of the wild section, where the hedge and an open space with a white cement bench formed a natural amphitheater hidden from the main paths, the cyvlossics had gathered.

Sterling sat on the bench, his silver coat gleaming in the filtered light. Honey lounged nearby, her golden fur catching the last rays of sunset. The green-eyed one materialized from the shadows like smoke given form. Prism's coat cycled through muted colors—deep blues and grays that spoke of serious business. And scattered around the edges, hiding in the vague afternoon shadows, at least six other cyvlossics that Frankie didn't recognize. All of them sitting in perfect silence, waiting.

Spike padded into the mix without hesitation. She took an open place in the front—her place? Frankie realized with a chill that this wasn't a casual gathering. This was a formal convocation.

Frankie shivered. A dozen giant heads swiveled to look at her.

"Frankie," Spike screech-growled. "Sit."

Frankie didn't sit—wouldn't be good for her butter yellow tea-party outfit, but she dropped to rest on her heels. Now she was the same height as most of them, her face much closer to their teeth. She shut her mouth.

Sterling spoke first, his voice carrying the measured tones of someone delivering a report.

"Three months," he said. "Ninety-seven reports. Zero acknowledgments."

Honey's tail lashed once, her voice as sweet as her coat but her words bitter. "He ran my report through a translator. It turned my analysis of Chen's anxiety into 'subject exhibits mood variability.'"

"His system reduces us to color codes," said Prism, her voice barely above a hiss. "We are so not mood rings."

"And last month, he tagged my dispatch 'low-monetary value' and told me to 'come back with bedroom secrets,'" said another.

"Orr did this?" Spike looked shocked. "Is he sick?"

"You're out of date," Honey said.

"It's the son," Prism said, practically spitting the word.

David.

The green-eyed one did spit. Then it said, "Doesn't listen; gives orders that contradict earlier orders."

"That break our code," said Sterling.

"Asshole," the green-eyed one said.

"Jade!" Honey said.

"Am I wrong?"

They all started talking at once. Spike spoke above them.

"Why?" she said.

That didn't shut them up.

"We don't know," Sterling said.

"Doesn't answer our messages," said Prism.

"Mad at us?" Honey said.

"Doesn't appreciate us," Jade sneered.

"Turfing us out," one of the cyvlossics near Frankie said.

"Can't be," Sterling said. "He still sends orders."

"Orders to pass along gossip." Honey shook her head. "Useless."

Prism's coat flashed angry orange for just a moment before settling back to rainbow. "Not useless. But he must be feeling the pressure."

"Pressure?" Sterling asked.

"Celeste," Prism said. "Said she'd pay him. For dirt."

The circle fell silent. Even the garden's ambient sounds seemed to fade—no chirping from the decorative insects, no rustle of wind through carefully placed foliage.

"He did ask," Honey said finally. "New order: Document 'behavioral anomalies' and 'intimate relationship dynamics' of assigned humans."

"Like we're spy drones," Jade added with visible disgust.

A dark cyvlossic Frankie hadn't seen before spoke up from the shadows. "Sheff has a gambling problem. David wants details."

"Mine has a chronic illness," another said. "Requested detailed medical observations."

The temperature in the circle seemed to drop several degrees.

"He needs the money?" Honey batted her ear, and then licked the dead bug off it.

"Wants power, fast," Jade said. "Wouldn't know what to do with it if he got it." Jade swiveled their head. "We all knew this day would come."

"I didn't," Prism said, the orange starting to fade.

"Later today," Sterling said, his voice heavy. "Voss is debuting new holo-midges. Defensive drones disguised as decorative insects. Like always, they need to be modified to not sense us. I tried to tell David."

"What did he say?" Spike asked.

Sterling's ears flattened. "Nothing."

The silence that followed was thick with shared frustration and growing anger.

"We're agents," Prism said finally. "Not pets. Not decorative accessories. Not blackmail tools. We're professionals who've been reduced to mood rings by someone who thinks he can improve on Konrad's system."

"Konrad always acknowledged our reports within twenty-four hours," Honey said. "Always. Even if it was just a single word."

"Ack," Jade said.

Spike looked askance.

"For acknowledged."

Prism licked her paw and wiped her brow. "Sometimes 'good work.' Something, to show us we mattered."

"David hasn't opened a report in six weeks," Honey said. "I know because I tagged the last one with a priority flag. It's still sitting in his queue, marked unread."

Spike's tail swished slowly, thoughtfully. "Options?"

"Stop reporting," Jade said. "See how long it takes him to notice."

"He won't," Sterling said flatly. "He thinks that dashboard he created is giving him everything he needs. Automated summaries generated by algorithms that wouldn't recognize actual intelligence if it bit them."

"We could report directly to Konrad," the dark cyvlossic offered.

"Konrad's out of the game," Prism said. "Told David sink or swim."

The circle fell silent again as each cyvlossic contemplated the chances they would all sink.

"There's another way," Spike said quietly.

Every pair of eyes turned to her.

"Leave."

Silence. Shock on Sterling's plush face.

"Oh, sure," Honey sneered. "Like you did."

"Worked for me." Spike shrugged. "And Sunshine."

That got a reaction. Prism popped up onto her feet, back almost arched. Honey hissed.

Sterling merely grunted. "Yes, Spike's right. Sunshine got away Cloud a year or so ago," the gray cyvlossic said. "No one seems to know how, and she's not saying. She's fine," Sterling continued, anticipating Prism's question. "Contacted me. Said to keep mum until she knew where she ended up. She checks in every few months." Sterling looked at Spike. "More than some others do."

Then Sterling's gaze swung past all the cyvlossics. "We vote," he said. "Stay or go."

"What would that mean?" Honey asked. "Practically speaking?"

"We stop reporting to David," Sterling said. "All of us. The network goes dark, from his perspective."

"Or," said Spike.

Now heads tilted, confused. "Or?" Blackie said.

"Or get a new handler. One who appreciates you."

"Like who?" Prism said. "Nobody knows about us."

Spike looked toward Frankie. "Maybe somebody does."

A dozen intent faces swiveled to consider Frankie. Who tried to look competent while squatting down in the forest while wearing a party dress.

"Not immediately relevant," the dark cyvlossic said.

"Bullshit it's not," Prism said. "Find out more, would you Spike?" She looked to Sterling. "Is this really a thing we do a formal vote on?"

Sterling's dark brows drew down. "Use the old send-file

basket, to Konrad," he said. "But don't send. Just leave the messages in draft. We can chat there." He looked at Spike. "Whatever new information we receive, I'll upload it there."

"Are we seriously thinking of doing this?" Honey asked. "Leaving?"

"About damn time," Jade said.

"What about our humans?" someone in the shadows asked.

"What about them?" the black cyvlossic said.

"We can't just leave them!"

"What, you're worried nobody will ever give you treats again?"

Prism sighed. "Or the spa. I'd miss the spa."

All their heads snapped to the right. Footsteps, one foot dragging slightly. The black cyvlossic vanished into the bush beside Frankie. For an animal as big as a large dog, it was creepily silent.

"Talk later " Sterling said, soft, as the cyvlossics melted away into the soft garden shadows, headed in different directions. By the time the gardener appeared at the edge of the clearing, clearly walking right on by, only Spike and Frankie remained.

Spike stood, stretched with deliberate casualness, and padded over to Frankie. She banged her head into Frankie's knee, performing affection for the audience of one. Frankie waved at the gardener but didn't stand up right away.

"You almost told them about Bruce!" Frankie hissed. Spike just flicked her tufted ears.

"Need to call the office tonight," she said.

But first they had to make it through the garden party. Standing, Frankie heard loud voices, officious. The speechifying had begun.

By the time they rejoined the party, the other cyvlossics had seamlessly returned to their positions. Sterling back at attention by the refreshments, Honey once again the perfect companion at Minister

Chen-Okoye's side, Prism cycling through pleasant blues and greens as she followed Bellemont. But they were still exchanging glances with one another, subtle signals passing between them.

They'd missed some story about the gardens. But now Senator Voss was coming up to the speaker's spot, in front of a arched arbor covered with golden heritage roses.

"Distinguished Citizens" Voss said, her voice carrying easily across the open space. "I want to share something rather special with you today. A small demonstration of the kind of innovation our defense contractors are bringing to personal security."

She reached into her pocket and withdrew what looked like a handful of bugs. Each no bigger than Frankie's thumb, obviously crafted with an attention to detail that made them seem almost alive.

"Holo-midges," Senator Voss announced with obvious pride. "The latest in discreet personal protection. Each one contains a full sensor suite, defensive countermeasures, and enough processing power to assess and respond to threats in real-time."

She activated one with a subtle gesture, and the tiny device rose into the air without a sound. Its zig-zag movements were eerily organic as it circled above her head.

"The beauty of the design," she continued, "is that they're virtually indistinguishable from decorative garden insects. Perfect for events like this, where traditional security might be… intrusive."

Around the crowd, people murmured appreciation. A few held out their hands expectantly, clearly hoping for a closer look. Sterling, positioned a little to the left of the senator, had gone absolutely still—the kind of stillness that suggested every instinct was screaming danger.

"I'd like each of you to take one as a party favor," Senator Voss said as her aides started going through the crowd distributing the devices. "Think of them as your personal security detail for the rest of the afternoon."

David Orr, standing at the edge of the crowd, accepted one of the devices with a polite smile. And then he looked at it, and scowled.

"Now," Senator Voss said, "let me show you how they work. Each midge performs continuous environmental scanning, looking for anything that might pose a threat to its assigned person."

"Scary," a guest said.

"Looks like synth-tech," another said.

"Nonsense," Voss replied. "Cooperative rules keep us safe from all that." She gestured, and her demonstration device began a more systematic patrol pattern, sweeping in careful arcs. "These are programmed to identify weapons, unusual electronic signatures, aggressive behavioral patterns—"

The device's flight pattern suddenly shifted. Instead of the leisurely patrol, it snapped into what was clearly an attack posture, diving toward the group around Minister Chen-Okoye.

Specifically, toward Honey.

"Fascinating!" Senator Voss said, apparently delighted. "It's detected something. Let's see what's triggered the alert."

The midge descended rapidly, its sensors focused on the golden cyvlossic. Honey, who had been peacefully sitting beside her minister, suddenly tensed. Her ears flattened against her head, and she made a sound Frankie had never heard from a cyvlossic before—a low, electronic whine that seemed to come from somewhere deeper than her throat.

"Honey?" Minister Chen-Okoye leaned down, concerned. "What's wrong, darling?"

The midge's scanning intensified, visible light patterns playing across its tiny form as it hovered directly over the cyvlossic. Sterling, across the garden, was moving now, abandoning his post to pad rapidly toward the commotion.

Honey's whine rose in pitch. She was pressed against Chen-Okoye's legs now, every line of her body suggesting terror.

"Well," the senator continued, "the midge is programmed to neutralize potential threats. Let's see what happens when—"

"Stop!" David said, but he was too late.

The midge discharged.

It wasn't loud—just a sharp crack like static electricity. But Honey collapsed instantly, her golden body hitting the manicured grass with a sound that seemed far too final.

For a moment, absolute silence.

"Honey!" Minister Chen-Okoye dropped to her knees beside her companion. "Honey, what—she's not breathing!"

Security appeared from seemingly nowhere, their gray dress uniforms a wave of motion. Guests scattered, some toward the commotion to help, others away from what might be danger.

Senator Voss stared at the chaos in apparent shock. "I don't understand. It should have been a minimal pulse, just enough to disable any electronics. It wasn't supposed to—"

"You killed her!" Minister Chen-Okoye's voice cracked with grief and fury. "You killed my Honey!"

David Orr pushed through the gathering crowd, his face cycling through expressions too quickly to track. When he reached the scene, he stared down at Honey's still form for a long moment.

"Just a malfunction," he said finally, his tone suggesting he was addressing a technical problem rather than a tragedy. "We'll get her repaired. These things happen with 'vlossics."

The words fell into the garden like boulders into still water.

Frankie watched in horrified fascination as every cyvlossic in the garden turned to stare at David. Sterling, who had reached the scene, looked at the man who was supposedly his handler with an expression that somehow conveyed utter contempt despite the limitations of feline features.

Prism, visible across the garden, had gone pink-white—not the shifting colors of normal emotional response, but the absolute absence of light that suggested something fundamental had broken.

Jade materialized from the shadows, no longer bothering to maintain the careful distance proper companions kept. She joined Sterling directly between David and Honey's twitching body, green eyes fixed on his face with predatory intensity.

"Repaired?" Minister Chen-Okoye's voice was barely controlled. "She's not a machine, you insensitive—"

"Actually," David interrupted, and Frankie saw the exact moment he realized his mistake, "I mean—what I meant was—"

But the damage was done. Around the garden, every cyvlossic was moving, abandoning their people to converge on the scene. They formed a protective circle around Honey's body, facing outward toward the humans.

Get. Away.

David Orr froze. He stared at the cyvlossics as if seeing them clearly for the first time.

Beth appeared at Frankie's elbow. "What just happened? Is Spike okay?"

Frankie watched the cyvlossics maintain their vigil, watched David's growing realization that something fundamental had shifted, watched Senator Voss fumble with her device as if she could somehow undo what it had done.

"I think," Frankie said quietly, "we just witnessed a revolution."

CHAPTER
TEN

AN HOUR LATER, Frankie was draped on one of the loveseats in her suite while Spike did her tech genius thing with the feed connection in the bedroom. Bruce hadn't answered right away so Spike was typing a message, grumbling all the while.

The door chimed, and Beth entered Frankie's suite in a whirlwind of jasmine and frustration, her political mask nowhere in sight.

"Thank gods you're here. I've been trying to escape for twenty minutes but the education minister just would not leave." She collapsed onto the opposite loveseat with zero grace. "What an absolutely bizarre afternoon."

"That's one way to put it."

"I mean, first all the cyvlossics disappear into the wilderness like they're having some kind of secret dance party, then they come back acting… different. And then poor Honey—" Beth's voice caught. "And David! What a creep."

Spike came out of the bedroom and jumped onto Frankie's loveseat, her front paws on Frankie's leg. Frankie held her arms out for a hug. Spike dropped onto her butt and started licking a paw. But Frankie knew what she wanted.

"How is she, do you know?" Frankie said.

"Not dead, at least. Seriously fried, apparently. Did you know the cyvlossics all go to the same vet? Luckily, she was on call."

"The poor girl definitely needs a day at that fancy spa," Frankie said.

"Don't we all." Beth trailed off, studying Frankie's face. "You disappeared right after they did. Before, into the wild section. Did you see what they were doing out there?"

Frankie glanced at Spike, who had gone still. "Probably just animal things. Sniffing butts."

"Mm." Beth's eyes narrowed slightly. "Animal things that had Sterling abandoning his post and Honey leaving a luxurious petting session?"

Sometimes Frankie forgot how sharp Beth was under all the political polish.

"The wedding's making everyone anxious," Frankie offered. "Even the pets."

"Especially the pets." Beth sighed, sinking deeper into the cushions. "I swear, every cyvlossic in the Complex has been acting strange. Jumpy. Clingy. The Regent's security chief thinks someone might be targeting them."

Spike's ears twitched.

"Targeting how?" Frankie kept her voice casual.

"Who knows? Poison, maybe. Or some kind of sonic thing that only they can hear." Beth waved a hand. "Security's paranoid about everything these days. Weddings bring out the worst in people sometimes."

"Are they worried someone will target Lucien?" The Regent's heir wasn't unpopular, but no one was universally loved.

"Heavens, no. Nobody wants the regency to go to the second son. Alain? Can you imagine? He'd turn the governmental buildings into vertical farms and make senators attend lectures on soil composition." Beth's expression softened. "Which is exactly why I love him, but not exactly leadership material."

"Good thing there's a third son."

"The best thing." Beth studied her for a moment. "How are you, really?"

"It's…" Frankie searched for words that were both true and incomplete. "Familiar. Like a shoe that used to fit."

"And now gives you blisters." Beth nodded. "I know. Even I feel it sometimes, and I chose to stay." She paused. "The others made the right choice, not coming."

"You talked to them?"

"Their polite rejections talked to me." Beth's smile was rueful. "Ellen didn't even bother with an excuse. Just 'unable to attend.' Joy at least wrote a whole paragraph about scheduling conflicts."

"They're happy," Frankie said quietly. "In their new lives."

"Good. Really." Beth stood, slipping her shoes back on with a grimace. "I should go. Dinner planning committee in twenty minutes. Tomorrow's the state dinner—the big one. Full formal, all the Great Houses, media in attendance."

Frankie's stomach dropped. "How formal?"

"The kind where they count the tines on your forks." Beth's expression was sympathetic. "I tried to get you excused, but the Regent insisted. Something about 'complete representation of Wala's legacy.'"

Of course. Because the wedding wasn't complete without trotting out all the orphans who were willing to show up.

"I'll put you next to Morgan," Beth promised. "He's good at distractions. And away from First Citizen Bellemont—she's been asking about you all afternoon."

AS AFTERNOON CLOSED TOWARD EVENING, Frankie initiated another of those Regent's purple super-high-security calls, this time to Morgan Orr. Same sofa as before, same screen, but this time Spike sat next to her, and Frankie was wearing her comfortable clothes. And nursing a mood-boosting juice concoction.

Morgan answered immediately, from what was apparently the sitting room side of his bedroom. Jackets in various states of color-change were draped over furniture, including the back of the fabric wingback chair he sat in. Small pyramids of actual books created navigation hazards.

"Sorry about the mess," he said, not sounding sorry at all.

"Thanks for picking up." Frankie had been worried that Celine was still there, but she didn't see evidence of it.

"That purple Regent's call banner is quite daunting." He grinned. "I was afraid what might happen if I said no."

"Are you alone?" Frankie asked.

Morgan's eyebrow waggled up and down. "You said you weren't feeling that way. Is that amazing looking juice giving you all the feels? Kidding! Yes, all alone. Just got home, in fact."

Good. "What's David's connection to the cyvlossics?" Frankie said.

Morgan looked down, toward the bottom of his screen, where the image of Spike would be.

"That's… unexpected," he said.

"You saw the weird meeting today," Frankie said. "In the bushes."

"What do you know?"

"They're spies for your family. No one knows. They report to your father."

Morgan leaned forward and dropped out of the picture for a moment. When he returned, the chiaroscuro tunic was off and he wore only a plain navy t-shirt. He threw himself back into the chair, slouching.

"You're out of date. David's took them over. But he doesn't think he needs them."

"He's not listening to them?"

"From the way he talks about it, I believe he doesn't even open the reports. He made some kind of dashboard that 'summarizes' everything. He's not the tech genius our father is."

"Could you get to the reports?"

"Sure." Morgan waved a long, manicured hand. "Just give me all David's security codes. And one of his eyes."

Ugh.

"From what I saw—Sterling, Honey, that black as night one—they're not happy."

"Midnight," Morgan said. "What? Are they planning some kind of strike? Walkout?"

Spike's ears flattened.

Morgan pursed his lips. "Might work. David thinks everything he touches has to turn immediately into revenue. Losing the network completely for a week might wake him up." He shook his head."Can't believe Dad spent decades perfecting that network and David just wants it for click-bait."

HE LOOKED AT HER, and for a moment the mask dropped completely. "I hate this place, Frankie. I hate what it does to people. What it's doing to David, trying to turn him into Dad."

"He doesn't have to become your father."

"Doesn't he?" Morgan's laugh was bitter.

"You've seen him. Trying so hard to be the heir Konrad wants. But he thinks dad got rich fast—with money—when he really got rich slow. With ideas. And spies."

"Your family is scary."

"You have no idea."

CHAPTER
ELEVEN

THE NEXT MORNING Beth and Frankie took a trip, alone. Almost.

The wheeled car, big enough for four but holding only three, hummed along the coastal road, and Beth was asleep before they'd cleared the Complex gates.

Frankie watched her friend's face relax in sleep, all the political polish melting away. Beth's head tilted against the window, and in the morning light she looked younger. Not young—they'd never be young again, not after Wala—but younger. Her simple but careful ponytail had started to slip, and her mouth was slightly open. Her gray "not a princess" tunic and loose pants were starting to wrinkle, but no one else was going to see.

The driver, a woman in Regent's security colors with arms like a wrestler, caught Frankie's eye in the mirror and smiled. "Distinguished Citizen Blais pushes herself too hard. Good she's getting rest."

"Does she visit the memorial often?" Frankie asked softly.

"First time in months. Been too busy with…" The driver

gestured vaguely at everything. The wedding, the politics, the careful dance of power.

They left the city's vertical sprawl behind, following a road that curved along the coastline. Here, finally, Frankie could see actual horizon. The sea stretched endlessly, a blue so different from the controlled fountains and pools of the Complex. Waves crashed against rocks with chaotic rhythm. No optimization, no perfection, just water doing what water did.

The climate changed too. Inside the Regent's dome, everything was regulated. Out here, real wind buffeted the transport. Real sun created actual shadows. The air probably even smelled different, though the transport's filtration wouldn't let her know.

Beth stirred as they slowed, blinking awake with the disorientation of someone who'd forgotten what day it was.

"Oh," she said, straightening. "I didn't mean to—"

"You needed it," Frankie said.

Beth finger-combed her hair back into submission, though the wind would destroy her efforts the moment they stepped outside. "I've been looking forward to showing you this. It's… well, you'll see."

The memorial sat on a flat-topped rock formation that jutted out toward the sea like a natural platform. The builders had tried to drill into it, Beth explained as they parked, but the rock had defeated every attempt. So they'd built on top instead, working with what couldn't be moved.

"Like grief," Beth said, then looked embarrassed. "Too metaphorical?"

"Little bit," Frankie agreed, but she smiled.

The caretaker met them at the entrance—a older woman with sun-weathered skin who looked like she actually spent time outside. "Distinguished Blais! Everything's ready. The plants are responding well to the new nutrients, and I've cleared the labyrinth for your private reflection."

"Thank you, Ebena." Beth's smile was warm, genuine. "This is my friend, Citizen Styles."

The caretaker's eyes widened slightly—everyone knew the name—but she recovered quickly. "An honor. The memorial is yours for as long as you need."

She withdrew to a cottage-like building near the parking area, but not before Frankie caught the look she exchanged with the driver. Quick, pitying. The kind of look people shared over well-meaning delusions.

No one else was here. No other transports in the lot, no visitors walking the paths. Just Beth's beautiful memorial, empty under the morning sun.

"Come on," Beth said, taking Frankie's arm. "I want you to see it properly."

The entrance was marked by a simple arch of Walan stone—rough, unpolished, the pale green color of deep lakes. Beyond it, the labyrinth spread in a perfect spiral, its paths marked by shoulder-high walls of growing things.

"Every plant is from Wala," Beth said, pride creeping into her voice. "Alain helped me track down the seed banks, negotiate with the botanical archives. That's actually how we met—I was trying to get permission to grow restricted species, and he was the only one who understood why it mattered."

The plants looked… struggling. Not dying, but clearly fighting. Their leaves were the wrong shade for Zichi's sun. Some curled at edges, others stretched desperately toward light that wasn't quite right. But they were alive. Still growing despite everything.

"Bugs love them," Beth continued as they approached the entrance. "We have to spray constantly or they'd be devoured. And the birds won't come near—something about the oils in the leaves. But they're surviving."

Like us, Frankie thought but didn't say.

The labyrinth path was smooth stone, wide enough for two to walk comfortable side by side. As soon as they entered, the sounds of sea and wind muffled. The plant walls created their own microclimate—humid, green, almost familiar.

"The idea," Beth said, already having to slow her naturally quick pace, "is contemplation. The path takes about twenty minutes if you don't rush. No choices to make, no shortcuts. Just… time to think."

"About what?"

"Whatever needs thinking about." Beth's voice went carefully neutral. "The plaque says something about patience and wisdom, but really it's about taking time. Not rushing into decisions that can't be undone."

Like firing an untested rocket too close to a planet. Frankie understood the message, even if she wasn't sure she agreed with it. Sometimes the problem wasn't rushed decisions. It was the people making them.

They walked in companionable silence for a while, following the spiral inward. Water channels appeared alongside certain sections, the water so clear it looked artificial. Which it probably was—recycled and filtered until all the life was cleaned out of it.

"I come here when I can," Beth said eventually. "Not as often as I'd like. But when things get too much, when the politics make me want to scream, I walk the path."

"Does it help?"

"Sometimes. Sometimes I just want to run through it, get to the center as fast as possible. But that defeats the purpose."

Frankie could see that—Beth forced to slow down, to be patient with her own creation. The meditation stones at each turn had phrases in High Galactic and Beth's Walan dialect, though the translations seemed too clean, too hopeful.

"'From patience, wisdom grows,'" Frankie read from one.

"Did we even have a word for patience? I remember Mama always rushing us places."

"It's more like 'thoughtful waiting,'" Beth admitted. "But that didn't sound as memorial-appropriate."

They kept walking, the spiral tightening. Frankie found herself oddly soothed by the forced pace, the lack of choices. Just follow the path, one foot in front of the other. The struggling plants released oils that did smell like home—sharp, green, with an undertone of something medicinal.

"The others aren't coming," Frankie said quietly. "Ellen and Joy. I tried, again, last night. They both said no. Again."

Beth's step hitched slightly, but she kept walking. "I know."

"You know?"

"You were trying to soften it. Make excuses. Like I'm too fragile to hear that Joy's furious with me and Ellen's forgotten we exist."

"Beth—"

"I'm not fragile, Frankie. I live in a nest of political vipers and make them think they're winning when I get what I want. I know exactly why Joy hates me."

"She doesn't hate you."

"She hates what I represent. What I chose. And she's not wrong." Beth's voice was steady, matter-of-fact. "I took our tragedy and used it. Built a career on it. She sees that as betrayal."

"And Ellen?"

"Ellen chose erasure. New name, new life, new identity. We're reminders of what she's running from." Beth paused at another meditation stone. "'In stillness, truth.' The truth is, sometimes people grow apart."

They were nearing the center now. Frankie could see something glinting through the final curves—metal catching sunlight.

"Can I ask you something?" Frankie said. "About Alain?"

"The age difference?" Beth smiled slightly. "Everyone wonders but only you would actually ask."

"Eleven years is—"

"Significant. I know. When I was learning to walk, he was already in secondary school. When I was dealing with..." She gestured at everything. "He was at university, falling in love with plants."

"Doesn't it feel strange?"

"No." Beth's answer was immediate, certain. "It feels like finding someone who existed outside all of this. He never knew me as the orphan. Never watched me perform grief for cameras. He just saw a woman trying to make dead seeds grow."

They rounded the final curve, and the center opened before them.

It was simple, which surprised Frankie. A circular plaza maybe ten meters across, paved with the same smooth stone. In the very center, the sword stood upright, point embedded in a rough block of Walan stone. Behind it grew a single tree— gnarled, ancient-looking, but green with new growth.

Around the tree's base, six smooth stones formed a circle. Each one different, unique. Four for the orphans, two for the chaperones who couldn't live with what they'd survived.

But it was the sword that drew Frankie forward.

Made of some alloy no one had ever seen before. Hidden, or dropped, or who knew what into a lake on the planet Wala, who knew when. Found on a hot summer's day by two girls playing in the water, not expecting to find something. Not expecting such a find would change everything.

Alien technology, they called it. Weird to call such a classical shape "technology." The find had earned Beth and Frankie and Erin and Joy and two chaperones a trip up to the new orbital station—Cooperative Realm territory. Walans weren't Cooperative citizens, and never could be. But people from so many other planets were on-station.

The girls giggled with giddy scientists, stood in awe of officious diplomats, and ate lots and lots of treats.

And, on the second day, watched their world be destroyed.

A supposedly errant test rocket built by Orr Industries got caught in the planet's gravity well. The implosion took less than fifteen minutes. Fifteen minutes, and they were orphans. Refugees. Wards of the Cooperative Realm.

"It's so exact," Frankie breathed, reaching out to touch the hilt. The metal was warm from sunlight, and her hand remembered. "Every detail."

"I had them scan the original twenty times," Beth said. "Drove the fabricators crazy. But I needed it right."

Frankie's fingers found the place where she'd gripped it, pulling it from the sand, from the water. "You kicked it."

"I stubbed my toe on it," Beth corrected. "Hard. I thought it was a root."

"You were hopping around cursing. I thought you were being dramatic."

"My toe was purple for a week!"

"You complained for two weeks."

They looked at each other across the memorial plaza, and suddenly it was funny. Hilarious. Two little girls fighting over who deserved credit for finding an ancient artifact while their families made dinner two hundred meters away.

"You said—" Beth was trying not to laugh. "You said I should get my eyes checked if I thought roots were made of metal."

"You said I should get my brain checked if I thought swords grew underground like potatoes."

"And then Professor Kemt showed up—"

"And we both tried to tell him at the same time—"

"And he wanted to give credit to Erik because he was the one who ran to get the grownups—"

They were both laughing now, real laughter that echoed off the stones. Frankie sank onto one of the benches, hugging herself. Beth joined her, tears streaming down her face.

"My six-year-old brother got credit for discovering proof of pre-human civilization," Frankie gasped. "He couldn't even pronounce 'archaeology.'"

"'Arky-loopy,'" Beth mimicked, and they dissolved again.

But the laughter shifted, as it always did. Because Erik was gone. Their families were gone. Everyone who'd heard this story first was gone. Except them.

"If we hadn't fought about it," Beth said quietly. "If we'd just reported it quickly instead of arguing for twenty minutes…"

"We might be dead too." Frankie's hand found Beth's, and squeezed. "That stupid argument saved our lives."

"It gave us these lives," Beth corrected. "I'm not sure that's the same thing."

They sat silent, looking at the sword that had changed everything. The tree rustled above them—real wind, not climate control. Somewhere beyond the labyrinth walls, gulls called.

"So you picked this date," Frankie said. "The anniversary."

"I thought I could transform it. Make it about beginnings instead of endings." Beth's laugh was hollow. "Alain thinks I'm being morbid. He's too polite to say so, but I can tell."

"Are you?"

"Maybe. Probably. But I can't seem to let go of it, you know? Every year it comes around and I think this time I'll be okay. And every year I'm not."

"So you're making it into a wedding."

"The ultimate transformation." Beth pulled her hand free, wrapping her arms around herself. "Joy thinks I'm erasing our grief. She's probably right."

"You're processing it. Just… very publicly."

"With flowers and cake and five thousand guests who'll pretend they're not thinking about the date's significance."

Frankie studied her friend. Really looked at her. The exhaustion beneath the polish, the way she held herself like armor against the world.

"Do you think they even care?"

"What?"

Frankie shrugged. "Some people like to forget. Some change the story. Some never cared in the first place. A lot, probably."

Beth sighed. "I *wish* the newsfeeds would forget." She waved a hand at the sword. "The Regent wants me to use it," she said. "The real one. For the ceremony."

Frankie's heart stilled. "What?"

"The Unity Blade ceremony. She thinks it would be meaningful—the sword that saved us, now blessing the succession." Beth's voice was carefully neutral. "Full circle, she called it."

"But it's in the university vault."

"Was. They're bringing it tomorrow. I'll present it to Lucien during the ceremony, showing that even we—the refugees— support the succession." She touched the replica, lightly, with her finger. "I haven't held the real one since… since that day with Professor Kemt."

"You don't have to—"

"Yes, I do." Beth's smile was tired. "It's an honor, remember? Everything here is an honor that you can't refuse."

She pulled her hand back. "Ready to head back? There's a shortcut."

"Of course there is."

Beth led her to what looked like solid hedge but was actually a concealed gate. "Safety feature. In case someone has a medical emergency or… other issues."

They emerged near the caretaker's building, bypassing the

entire return journey. The metaphor was too obvious to mention
—Beth creating elaborate paths and then building in ways to
avoid them.

"Thank you for coming," Beth said as they walked toward the
transport. "For seeing it. No one else—" She stopped. "I mean,
it's been a while since I could show someone who'd understand."

Frankie heard what she wasn't saying. No one else comes.
This beautiful memorial to their lost world, and she was probably
the first visitor besides Beth in months.

"It's beautiful," Frankie said, and meant it. "Different than I
imagined, but beautiful."

"Different how?"

"I thought it would be angrier."

"I tried angry. The first design had broken stones and wilting
plants and quotes about justice." Beth climbed into the transport.
"But anger gets exhausting. And it doesn't bring them back."

"Neither does beauty."

"No. But at least beauty I can stand to visit."

The driver started back toward the city, and this time Beth
stayed awake. They watched the sea give way to suburbs, then
the vertical sprawl of the capital. Real wind replaced by climate
control. Chaos replaced by order.

"My door is open," Frankie said quietly as the Complex gates
came into view.

"My hand is yours," Beth finished. "Even when we're all
choosing different things."

"Even then."

The memorial would stay empty. The struggling plants would
keep fighting Zichi's wrong sun. The sword would stand in its
perfect plaza, waiting for visitors who wouldn't come.

But for one morning, two women had walked the labyrinth
their younger selves never could have imagined needing. They'd

laughed about a childhood argument that saved their lives. They'd cried for everyone who hadn't been so lucky.

And maybe that was enough. Maybe that was all any memorial could really do—give the living a place to remember and release, to hold on and let go.

As they pulled up to the Complex, Beth squeezed Frankie's hand once, quickly.

"See you at the state dinner," she said, mask sliding back into place. "Try not to stab anyone with the fish fork."

"That was one time," Frankie protested. "And he deserved it."

"Senator Hadris still has the scar."

"Good."

Beth laughed, bright and political and real all at once. "I'm glad you're here. Whatever else happens, I'm glad."

"Me too," Frankie said, and was surprised to find she meant it.

CHAPTER
TWELVE

THE CEREMONIAL ATTIRE arrived in a hovering case of polished silver. No tailor this time, just an impersonal delivery with the Regent's seal glowing on top. The case settled on Frankie's bed with the quiet confidence of something that knew its own importance.

"What is it?" Frankie asked the empty room. Spike, who had been dozing on the window seat, opened one eye.

"Trouble," she rasped.

The case unsealed itself with a soft hiss, revealing layers of midnight blue fabric shot through with silver threads that caught the light like trapped stars. Frankie's breath caught. She knew this dress. Not this specific one, but its kind—the formal attire of a Walan diplomatic representative.

She hadn't worn anything like it since she was sixteen.

A small card nestled among the fabric, its cream surface embossed with the Regent's seal:

For tonight's State Dinner, the Regent requests all Wala representatives honor their heritage.

Not a request. A command.

"She's weaponizing our past," Frankie muttered, lifting the main piece from its nest. The fabric felt impossibly light yet substantial, engineered to move beautifully while protecting the wearer from environmental variables—or at least, that had been the original design philosophy. Now it was purely ceremonial, the protective elements replaced by decorative ones.

The silver embroidery depicted Wala's night sky as it had appeared from the capital city, major constellations picked out in tiny crystals. A view that no longer existed except in memory and archive.

Frankie laid it across the bed, fingers trailing over the traditional patterns. The matching shoes. The silver circlet meant to rest at her temples. Everything precisely as protocol dictated.

"They really don't want us forgetting what we're here for, do they?" she said to Spike.

The cyvlossic stretched, back arching impossibly.

Frankie sighed, then squared her shoulders. She could do this. One more formal dinner, one more performance.

Every ceremonial clasp clicked like a cuff, locking her back into the day the newsfeeds crowned her "The Face of Survival." The door chimed as she was fastening the last of the clasps, at her shoulder.

"It's open," she called.

Morgan entered, and for once, Frankie found herself speechless. Gone was the color-changing disaster of previous events. Instead, he wore formal attire that complemented hers—midnight blue with silver accents, though his bore the subtle markings of the Orr family rather than Walan symbols.

"They got to you too," she said, finding her voice.

"Regent's office sent it over this morning. Apparently, we're all playing our parts tonight." He tugged at the high collar. "Though I think they underestimated my neck circumference."

"You look…" Frankie searched for the right word.

"Respectable? Dashing? Like I might actually belong to my family?"

"I was going to say 'uncomfortable,' but sure, those too."

Morgan grinned, then sobered as he took in her appearance. "Walan formal diplomatic attire. That's… pointed."

"Very." Frankie adjusted the circlet at her temples. It felt foreign and familiar all at once, like a language she'd once been fluent in but had deliberately forgotten. "So clear that this isn't the 'friendly family gathering' from last time. This is pure theater."

"Complete with program notes." Morgan held up a narrow tablet. "Tonight's proceedings, all eighty-four meticulously scheduled minutes of them. We have speaking roles."

"We what?" Frankie grabbed the tablet, scrolling quickly. There it was, under "Ceremonial Acknowledgments": Representatives of Wala to offer traditional blessing. "They can't be serious."

Morgan took the tablet back. "The Regent's pulling out all the diplomatic stops for this one. Every major political player, delegation representatives from seven systems, media coverage—though tastefully restricted to approved feeds, of course."

Spike made a noise somewhere between a growl and a snort.

"What about you?" Frankie asked her. "Pet dress code?"

Spike fixed her with a withering stare. Actually, she still looked pretty good from her time at the pet spa—despite the fact that cyvlossics were not pets. Just a little ruffling of the belly fur, but the back and ears still seemed fairly respectable.

Frankie checked the time. "We should go. According to the schedule, we're expected to join the processional in…" She grimaced. "Eight minutes."

Morgan offered his arm with exaggerated formality. "Shall we face the lions, Representative Styles?"

She took it, grateful for the friendly touch amidst all the cold ceremony. "Just promise you won't let me stab anyone with the ceremonial cutlery. No matter how tempting."

"Not even David?"

"...Maybe David."

THE PROCESSIONAL ROUTE wound through sections of the Complex that Frankie had never seen open before. Ancient corridors with vaulted ceilings, their walls embedded with historical markers and ceremonial artifacts. The floor beneath their feet changed from the usual polished composite to what looked like stone but couldn't possibly be—no one transported actual stone between worlds anymore, not when synthetics were lighter and more durable.

Except, perhaps, for ceremonial routes walked only on the most significant occasions.

"When was the last time they actually used this section?" Frankie whispered to Morgan as they waited in the precisely arranged line of dignitaries.

"The Regent's ascension ceremony, thirty-five years ago," he murmured back. "It's been a meeting spot for all the tour groups since then."

Ahead of them, the line moved forward in perfect time to the ceremonial music filtering through hidden speakers. Each guest or delegation was announced, their titles and affiliations echoing through the ancient space. The gap between announcements was precisely twelve seconds—enough time for the previous party to clear the entrance before the next was called.

Frankie's palms were sweating. She wiped them surreptitiously on the midnight fabric, grateful that it was engineered to repel moisture.

"Distinguished Citizens Morgan Orr and Francesca Styles, representing the Orr family interests and the Wala Diaspora."

Morgan squeezed her arm gently as they moved forward. "Breathe."

They stepped through the massive doorway into the Grand State Hall, and Frankie had to force herself not to stop and stare.

This place was a cathedral to power. Triple-height ceilings soared overhead. Hidden lights shone on dozens of banners from family houses alive and long gone that hung in perfectly preserved splendor. The floor was inlaid with a map of the original seven Cooperative worlds, their positions marked in precious metals and stones. The tables were arranged in a ceremonial star pattern, each point representing a major political faction, with the Regent's position at the center.

Hell for security.

Hundreds of guests already had arrived, each in formal attire that signified their world, their faction, their status. The air was heavy with ceremonial incense burning in ancient holders, the scent designed to evoke the original signing of the Cooperative charter.

Morgan guided her forward, following the attendant who led them to their assigned positions. As representatives of both Orr interests and Wala, they were seated at one of the secondary tables—not at the Regent's central star, but close enough to signify importance.

Frankie recognized their table placement immediately. The Wala position. A place of honor tinged with performative sympathy. Had the other survivors attended, they would have been placed separately at strategic intervals around the hall, visual reminders of the Cooperative's mercy and generosity.

"Breathe," Morgan whispered as they took their seats. "You look like you're about to snap that ceremonial wine glass in half."

Frankie forced her fingers to relax. "I feel like I'm sixteen again, being trotted out for the cameras."

"Tonight, we're all being trotted out." Morgan nodded subtly toward the media drones positioned discreetly around the perimeter. "Just be grateful they put us together. I requested it specifically."

"You did?"

"Told them it was a cultural sensitivity issue. That Wala survivors prefer familiar support persons during ceremonial events." His eyes twinkled. "Made it up completely, but they bought it."

For the first time since the silver case arrived, Frankie felt herself relax slightly. "My hero."

The hall fell silent as the massive bronze ceremonial gong was struck once, its resonance filling the space. Frankie had to force herself not to cover her ears, the thing was so loud.

The Regent entered from a private door near the central position, her formal attire putting everyone else's to shame. The high collar of her gown mimicked the crystalline structures of the mining colonies, while the flowing sleeves borrowed the sweeping lines of desert world garments. The bodice incorporated the metallic weave unique to the orbital stations, and the skirt's deep indigo carried the precise shade of the ancient maritime powers. Even her jewelry made statements—earrings of agricultural circuit patterns, a necklace featuring the sacred geometric forms of the spiritual enclaves.

Every element deliberately chosen, meticulously integrated, a walking political tapestry. Her presence drew every eye, her posture conveying absolute confidence in her right to command this space.

She took her place at the center, not sitting yet—no one would sit until she did—and surveyed the gathered dignitaries with measured satisfaction.

"Welcome," she said, her voice perfectly modulated to reach every corner of the hall without seeming to project. "Tonight we gather not merely for a meal, but for a recommitment to the principles that bind our worlds together. Peace. Prosperity. Unity."

Her gaze swept the room, lingering briefly on the Wala table. On Frankie.

"Tonight we also celebrate the joining of two great families, a union that strengthens us all. Distinguished Citizen Blais and Distinguished Citizen diCimino represent the best of our values —service, loyalty, vision."

Alain and Beth stood at the Regent's left. Beth's gown made Frankie's heart twist with recognition. The base fabric shimmered with the distinctive copper-infused weave that had been Wala's primary export, while the cut followed traditional lines—high-necked, close-fitted through the bodice, with a draped overlay that suggested the ceremonial robes of the southern provinces. But subtle modifications spoke of her new identity: the sleeves bore the tight pleating favored by Capital politicians, the sash at her waist displayed the exact shade of diplomatic purple used in official communications, and her hair was arranged in the intricate braided style that marked high-ranking advisors to the Regent.

Even her jewelry balanced between worlds—simple copper bands at her wrists for Wala, and at her throat, the delicate silver chain of a Distinguished Citizen. Alain looked both honored and slightly bewildered by the formality of it all, his own attire clearly chosen for him rather than by him.

"And we anticipate," the Regent continued, "the return of First Citizen diCimino from his diplomatic mission, completing our circle as we begin these celebrations."

On cue, the ceremonial gong sounded again. A lighter strike, easier on the ears, the traditional announcement of an heir's arrival.

First Citizen Lucien diCimino stepped through the massive doors, and even Frankie—who prided herself on her immunity to political theater—felt the impact of his presence.

He wore the traditional colors of succession—deep red and gold—with the symbolic stars of leadership on his collar. His dark hair was cropped close in military fashion, emphasizing the sharp diCimino cheekbones and strong jaw. He moved with the practiced grace of someone who had spent years learning how to appear relaxed while remaining combat-ready.

But it was his eyes that caught Frankie's attention. Dark like his brother's, but lacking Alain's open warmth. These were the eyes of someone who had seen too much and trusted too little.

Lucien acknowledged each political faction with precise, calculated gestures as he made his way toward the central star, the media drones hovering like gnats an arm's length away from him. When he reached his brother and Beth, he performed the ceremonial greeting flawlessly—taking Beth's hand with just the right pressure, inclining his head at just the right angle. Perfect protocol, but Frankie caught something genuine in the respectful nod he gave her.

Then he turned to the Regent, executing the formal bow of an heir to the current leader. The Regent acknowledged him with the traditional response, and only then did she finally take her seat, signaling everyone else to do the same. The media gnats whirred toward the walls.

The ceremonial chimes marked the beginning of the meal service.

"Well," Morgan murmured as the first course was served with balletic precision by synchronized attendants, "that was suitably dramatic."

"Is he always like that?" Frankie asked quietly, watching as Lucien engaged in formal conversation with the dignitaries at the central star.

"Lucien? Yes and no. The ceremonial perfect heir is definitely a performance, but the military precision is real enough. He did ten years in the Cooperative Defense Force before being recalled to succession duties."

Frankie studied Lucien more carefully. Now that he was seated, she could see subtle indicators Morgan's observation had missed. The way he positioned himself at the table, sight lines always clear. The way his attention remained divided between the conversation and his surroundings. The almost imperceptible scan he performed each time a server approached.

"He's expecting trouble," she murmured.

"Wouldn't you?"

Before Frankie could respond, one of their table companions —a diplomatic representative from one of the inner systems— leaned toward them with polite interest.

"First time at a state dinner?" she asked, her translator badge ensuring her words came through in perfect High Galactic despite her native language being something else entirely.

"First in many years," Frankie replied diplomatically.

"It is an honor to meet a survivor of Wala," the diplomat continued. "Your world's contributions to our cultural heritage are still celebrated."

Frankie gave the traditional response, her tongue remembering the formal phrases even as her mind rebelled at the sanitized version of history they represented. The diplomat seemed satisfied, turning the conversation to the ceremonial significance of the first course.

As the meal progressed through its elaborately choreographed courses, Frankie found herself falling into the rhythm of diplomatic small talk, a skill she'd thought long forgotten. Morgan provided subtle support, redirecting conversations when they veered too close to difficult topics, amplifying Frankie's points when political weight was needed.

But part of her attention—and everyone else's—remained on the central star, where the real power conversations were happening. The Regent presided with calculated graciousness, Beth performed her political role flawlessly, and Lucien, at the Regent's right hand, maintained his perfect balance of heir-apparent dignity and military alertness.

It was during the fourth course—a dish representing the mineral-rich world of Hargan, its components arranged to mimic the famous crystal formations—that Frankie noticed the cyvlossics.

They weren't seated at the tables, of course. Even companion animals, even prestigious ones like cyvlossics, remained at the perimeter of the hall. But they weren't positioned randomly. Sterling, Senator Voss's silver-gray cyvlossic, had positioned himself with clear sight-lines to where Honey sat near the media section. Prism, First Citizen Bellemont's color-shifting beauty, had migrated to a spot where she could see both Sterling and Jade, who lurked in the shadows near the service entrance.

A pattern. Not obvious unless you were looking for it, but unmistakable once spotted. The cyvlossics weren't watching their owners. They were watching one another.

The ceremonial gong sounded again, marking the transition to the formal addresses. The Regent rose, and all conversation ceased instantly.

"As we share this meal in the tradition of our ancestors," she began, "we also look to our future. The joining of Distinguished Citizen Blais and Distinguished Citizen diCimino represents more than a personal union. It symbolizes our continued commitment to integrating diverse perspectives into our leadership."

Political speak for "we occasionally let orphans marry into power," Frankie thought, but kept her expression neutrally pleasant.

"As part of this commitment to tradition and future, we are reviving the ancient Unity Blade ceremony."

Frankie's attention sharpened.

"Not merely symbolic, but a sacred trust—the blade that united our worlds will unite our families." The Regent gestured, and Beth and Lucien rose from their seats. "Distinguished Citizen Blais will present the Unity Blade to First Citizen diCimino, demonstrating the trust between our houses and the strength of our shared vision."

Beth's smile was perfect, her posture expressing the exact right balance of honor and humility. But Frankie, who knew her better than almost anyone, caught the momentary tightness around her eyes.

Frankie glanced toward Sterling and saw the cyvlossic had shifted position, his attention now divided between Lucien and the Regent. Across the hall, other cyvlossics had made subtle adjustments as well.

"The ceremony will take place during the wedding itself," the Regent continued, "but tonight, we formally announce this revival of our most sacred tradition."

The ceremonial chimes marked the end of her address, and the hall filled with the traditional response, hundreds of voices speaking in unison: "As it was, so shall it be."

As the formal toasts began, Morgan leaned close to Frankie. "Did you see the cyvlossics?"

"Yes," she murmured back. "Something's happening."

"David noticed too. Look."

Frankie casually glanced toward David Orr's position, at the next table. His expression was controlled, but his attention was fixed on Sterling with unmistakable suspicion.

"Think he knows?" she asked.

"No idea. But he knows something's not right." Morgan accepted a ceremonial toast cup from a passing attendant.

The remainder of the dinner passed in a murmur of ceremonial exchanges and carefully orchestrated conversations. Frankie performed her expected role, including the traditional Walan blessing that she had to drag from the recesses of her memory. All the while, her mind worked on the puzzle of the Unity Blade and the cyvlossics' unusual behavior.

As the Regent finally rose to signal the dinner's conclusion, Frankie caught sight of First Citizen Bellemont speaking intently with a young, beautiful woman with a bevy of drones around her, their conversation just beyond hearing range. Bellemont's cyvlossic, Prism, had positioned herself to overhear every word.

The formal procession out of the hall began, each faction departing in order of precedence. As Frankie and Morgan waited their turn, David Orr approached, his expression carefully neutral.

"Citizen Styles," he said, formal and cold. "I trust you found the evening educational."

"Deeply," Frankie replied with equal formality.

His gaze flicked to where Sterling was now positioned near the exit. "Interesting how the companion animals seem so… attentive tonight."

"All that ceremonial incense probably has them on edge," Morgan said lightly.

David's eyes narrowed slightly. "Are you in contact with them?"

"Of course not! That's your job." Morgan held a hand to his heart. "I'm so jealous."

"Danderbrain."

"Name-caller."

"Boys," Frankie said, signaling with her gaze the nearby media drone. They both shut up.

As they waited to be called for their ceremonial exit, Frankie watched the happy couple and the heir performing their formal farewells near the central star. Beth's political mask was perfect, Alain was doing his best. Lucien's attention kept shifting to the perimeter where the cyvlossics prowled.

CHAPTER
THIRTEEN

THE UNITY CHAPEL always took Frankie's breath away, even though she'd taken a car instead of walking up the six hundred unforgiving rock steps to get here. Anchored into the same massive rock formation as the memorial garden, the chapel sat alone, away from the bustle of the capital city, even though it was only technically a half-hour's walk from the Complex.

Nothing impeded its view of the vast ocean in the far distance, nor of the Regent's Complex nearer to hand. City building codes had kept the sightline to the Complex clear, but over the generations it had become a shadowed tunnel rather than a wide vista. Sturdy white solar siding and mirror-like windows gave the chapel a nondescript outer shell, easy for the wind to slide around. Inside told a different tale.

The vaulted space soared overhead, the ceiling so high that the elaborate frescoes depicting the founding of the Cooperative seemed to float in another atmosphere entirely. Sunlight poured through clear or frosted clerestory windows, casting perfect golden beams that illuminated certain areas while leaving others in dramatic shadow. The effect was calculated to highlight the ceremonial path between the aisles of fancy bench seating and the central dais, but the timing changed with the seasons. Which was why tomorrow's wedding was a ten o'clock sharp.

The light was sliding off the path now, catching just the edge of the deep purple carpet runner. Frankie stepped onto the runner and into the sun, and, for a moment, pretended to be a princess.

And then laughed.

The air carried traces of ceremonial incense probably embedded in the sand-brick walls, mingling with the potted flowers and air blooms being arranged for tomorrow's ceremony. There would be no dead flowers at this event.

The acoustics were legendary; Frankie could hear the soft footsteps of workers at the far end of the chapel as clearly as if they were walking beside her. And her own steps, crackling the plastic cover protecting the carpeting.

A florist hurried past carrying an armload of those strange Wala bell-flowers, nearly colliding with a media tech who was arguing into his comm about optimal hologram angles. The chapel's acoustics carried fragments - '…told you the purple would clash with…' '…need three more drones for coverage…' - creating a low hum of bustle and worry beneath the sacred space's usual tranquility.

Beth and Alain sat together in the front pew, reviewing details. Beth's snow white tunic over slim dark slacks looked deceptively simple. Alain, in contrast, wore what appeared to be khaki gardening clothes, complete with soil under his fingernails, and bounced between intense concentration and childlike distraction.

"Twenty-four hours from now, we'll be wed," he was saying as Frankie approached. "Hard to believe it's finally here."

Beth's expression softened momentarily. "If we survive the ceremony."

"The flowers will be perfect, at least." Alain smiled at Frankie and stood, gesturing excitedly at the elaborate arrangements being placed at the ends of the pews and along the round white columns supporting the high ceiling. "The symbolism is perfect—these bloom patterns represent unity in Hargan culture, and these —" he pointed to delicate purple blossoms "—are descended from Wala stock. I had them cultivated specially."

The mention of Wala caught Frankie off guard. She had never seen flowers like these, each stalk carrying a dozen bell-like flowers.

"South Wala," Beth added, giving Frankie a wobbly smile. They were both from one of the northern continents. "Welcome to the circus."

"Seems pretty quiet to me," Frankie said. "Tranquil."

"In your dreams."

"How can I help?"

"You can help me keep him focused," Beth said, nodding toward Alain, who had already wandered off to examine the vine carvings on a pillar. "The Protocol Minister will be here any minute."

Frankie followed Beth's gaze around the hall, taking in details her childhood self had never noticed. Facial scanners disguised as decorative elements. Pressure plates beneath the ceremonial carpets. Atmospheric sensors in the ancient vents. All nearly invisible unless you knew what to look for.

In this fortress of tradition and security, infiltration seemed almost laughably impossible. Perhaps everyone was overreacting after all. The cyvlossics' behavior, Spike's warnings, her own persistent unease—maybe it was all just wedding jitters amplified by the political stakes.

"Distinguished Citizen Blais," a clipped voice announced from the entrance. "Distinguished Citizen diCimino."

The Protocol Minister had arrived. Tall and rail-thin, her blond hair pulled back so tightly it seemed to function as a face-lift, she swept toward them in formal cream-and-blue long robes, datapad in hand.

"Citizen Styles," she added with less enthusiasm. "I see you've brought no companion animal today."

"Spike's resting," Frankie said neutrally. In truth, Spike was missing, having mentioned something about reconnaissance at breakfast. Or another trip to the spa.

"Very well. We have precisely forty minutes to perfect the section of the ceremonial proceedings." The protocol minister's stylus tapped her datapad with military precision. She did not give them her name. "Places, please."

Twenty weary minutes later, they had traveled from the foot of the walkway to the white-marble dais itself.

"Distinguished Citizen Blais, you will stand here." The protocol minister, frowning, positioned Beth on a circular inlay of polished black marble at the center of the dais. "Distinguished Citizen diCimino, you're here." She guided Alain to a position one step ahead and to the right of Beth.

Frankie tore two more pieces of bright green tape off the roll the minister had given her, sticking one strip at the point of Beth's formal dress shoes and another at the tip of Alain's flat garden sandals. The neon green wouldn't show up on the official recording cameras, apparently. Frankie sure hoped not—she'd already made X's and lines all over the place.

"First Citizen diCimino and I will sit here," the minister continued, pointing to the first pew on the right, Alain's side. "You can look to me for advice, which you should not need after this session." Beth nodded, and then winked at Frankie. Officials were going to be officious.

"The Regent will observe from this position." The minister indicated an elevated area to the right side of the dais, a space that looked open but really was surrounded on three sides by clear safety glass. Opposite the Regent's box stood the white marble lectern where the weekly services were led.

The dais itself was a marvel of local craftsmanship. Intricate symbols inlaid in precious metals and stones created a map of the Cooperative's first five worlds, with Alain's position at the very center. Beth would step back to join him at the center of their worlds.

Beth absorbed the instructions with complete focus, her body already attuned to the exact angles and distances required. Alain tried earnestly to follow along but kept getting distracted by the architectural details.

"Distinguished Citizen, please," the protocol minister said with thinly veiled exasperation. "Your position is of critical diplomatic importance."

"Sorry!" Alain said cheerfully. "But did you see the carved flora on those pillars? They're extinct now. Someone reproduced them with remarkable accuracy. Maybe they weren't extinct then."

The protocol minister's expression suggested she might be contemplating extinction herself. "We are practicing a ceremony that has occurred only seventeen times in the Cooperative's history. It would behoove you to pay attention."

"Sure, sure." Alain obediently returned to his mark, though his eyes continued to wander.

Frankie suppressed a smile. She could see why Beth loved him. In a world of calculated moves and political chess, Alain's genuine enthusiasm was refreshingly real.

From her position near the edge of the dais, Frankie noticed Morgan slipping into the hall. He positioned himself discreetly against a pillar, his formal outfit from last night replaced with something more practical. His subtle nod acknowledged her, but he remained at a distance, observing.

"Now," the protocol minister announced, "The Unity Blade. This comes after the homily and precedes the actual vow exchange."

At her signal, two assistants in Cooperative goldenrod approached from the side, carrying a black case that looked like it could hold a telescope or a very thin violin. They placed it on a designated stand and stepped back with ceremonial precision.

Passing behind them, a constant stream of activity. A security officer murmuring urgently into their comm, a junior protocol assistant color-matching ribbon samples against holographic projections of the Hargan delegation's formal wear, two florists in heated but whispered debate about whether air blooms should face the center aisle or the walls.

"The Unity Blade," the protocol minister intoned, "represents the binding of our worlds, the strength of our unity, the sharpness of our purpose." She entered a code on a small panel on top of the case, and it unsealed with the soft hiss of preservation gases.

Frankie leaned forward despite herself.

The sword from Wala, looking a lot less dingy than when she'd had hold of it, all those years ago. Not pitted at all. Frankie wondered at that—the metal composite was one no one had ever seen before. How had they smoothed it out?

Elegant in its simplicity, the sword was a single piece of silver-gray metal crossed by a darker gray, its hilt wrapped by what looked like round strands of metals melted or pounded into shape. It gleamed dully in the soft light, but step into the sun and it would shimmer silver-green.

"We normally use a blade from the First Regent," the minister said. "This one looks much like."

Frankie held back a snort. Nothing in their many worlds looked like this blade. Made by who knew who, and so long ago that the scientists had argued about the dating for a decade. Proof that the people of their worlds were not alone. Or hadn't been alone, all that time ago.

"Distinguished Citizen Blais," the protocol minister directed, "Take three measured steps toward the blade."

Beth stepped forward, but her stride wasn't long enough.

"Try again."

Still short.

The minister conferred with her assistants. They slid the stand a half-step closer to Beth. The minister waved at Frankie, and pointed to the floor. Frankie stuck another piece of the neon tape down.

This time, Beth's stride was perfect. She positioned herself before the case, hands at her sides.

"You will lift the blade thus." The protocol minister demonstrated without touching it, showing the precise angle and grip. "The ceremonial words must be spoken as you raise it, not before, not after."

Beth nodded, then carefully lifted the blade. "I lift this blade not in—"

The sword twisted in her grip, catching the light at an angle that sent a blinding flash directly into the protocol minister's eyes.

"Distinguished Citizen!" the minister said, blinking rapidly.

"Sorry! It just—" Beth adjusted her grip, and the blade flashed again, this time hitting one of the media techs setting up a holocam in the corner. The tech stumbled backward with a yelp. "It's like it has opinions about where to point."

Frankie remembered that sensation from when she was eight. The blade seeming to have its own ideas about balance and direction. Apparently the clear aluminum coating hadn't changed that.

"Control the ceremonial object, please," the minister said tersely, still blinking away spots.

Alain laughed. "Maybe it likes you!"

"The blade was recoated to preserve it," the minister said, as if this explained everything. "Clear aluminum. Perhaps that altered its balance."

Beth tried again, this time shading the blade slightly with her body. "I lift this blade not in challenge but in trust," she recited, her voice taking on the formal cadence required, "to bind our houses as it bounds our worlds."

This time the blade merely glimmered.

Four steps, a step off the dais, three steps to where the Lucien would sit. Frankie stood in for Lucien, standing at the moment Beth stepped off the dais.

Beth practiced the presentation several times, each movement critiqued and refined by the protocol minister. The hands at one-third and two-thirds, with the blade's true edge facing toward herself and pointing just slightly upward.

"Don't bow!" the minister said.

Between attempts, workers continued their preparations around them, adjusting light filters high up on the columns, setting even more flower displays on the dais. Twice the minister had to pause while media drones buzzed around them, their operators testing sight lines. One drone got so close to the minister's head, probably looking for the best face shot of Beth, that the minister swatted it like a bug. Its operator groaned as the little flying blob hit the ground.

Finally, Beth performed the steps to the minister's approval, holding the blade out to Frankie with perfect form. Frankie accepted it, taking the hilt in one hand and the blade flat in her palm equidistant between Beth's hands. For a moment, she was surprised by its perfect balance. The hilt fit her hand as if designed for it, the blade extending like a natural extension of her arm. It had done that when she was eight, and it did it again, despite her longer reach and stronger arm. Some weird kind of magic. She lifted it straight up. For a moment, she felt all powerful.

"Citizen!" The protocol minister hissed. "Not like that."

"Who handles the security for something so valuable?" Alain asked, head tilted as if he were trying to read some sort of writing on the blade..

The protocol minister's expression tightened slightly. "That information is restricted to those with clearance, Distinguished Citizen."

Alain merely grinned. "Okay. I'll ask Mom later."

The protocol minister shuddered. Nowhere in the all the scores of treatises on Cooperative etiquette did it ever advise calling The Regent mom.

"I do know that enhanced electronic countermeasures have been installed throughout the venue."

"Not those bugs from the garden party?" Alain asked, his expression shifting from cheerful to concerned.

"Precisely," the Protocol Minister replied crisply. "We cannot have companion animals being affected by stray signals during the ceremony. The countermeasures will prevent any similar technological interference."

Frankie set the blade carefully back onto her palm, and turned to her right. Tomorrow, Lucien would slide the blade into a blocked velvet sheath held by the protocol minister herself. Today, the sheath was held by another of her assistants.

As the protocol minister closed the case, Frankie felt a momentary relief. The security was comprehensive, the ceremonial details meticulously planned. Perhaps everyone really was overreacting.

As if.

The protocol minister called for another repetition, from the top, this time with the full musical accompaniment. As the ancient harmonies filled the space, Frankie felt the hairs on the back of her neck rise. Not from the music, beautiful as it was, but from the growing sense that she was missing something crucial.

The crash, when it came, shattered the ceremonial atmosphere like a stone through glass.

Beth had just reached the moment of blade presentation when a tremendous clatter erupted from the eastern entrance. A security guard had somehow knocked over an entire rack of ceremonial staffs, sending them cascading across the ancient stone floor with acoustics-amplified cacophony.

Beth flinched—a completely natural reaction—and the replica blade tilted in her grip, nearly slipping from her hands.

Four tan-and-gold-clad guards immediately surrounded the unfortunate staff-dropper, while others moved to secure the entrances.

"Return to first positions," the protocol minister ordered, seemingly oblivious to the security brouhaha. "We will begin again from the approach sequence."

Frankie watched with growing unease as Beth once again performed the blade presentation flawlessly. The beauty of the ceremony, the perfect acoustics, the historical significance—all of it should have been impressive, meaningful.

Instead, it felt increasingly like elaborate stage dressing for something else entirely.

"Acceptable," the protocol minister declared as the final notes of the ceremonial music faded. "Distinguished Citizens, I am proud to say you have mastered the basics of a tradition dating back four centuries."

Beth sighed deeply. "We'll do our best."

Alain wrapped an arm around her shoulders, his usual distraction replaced by quiet support. "Twenty-four hours, and then we're married. It doesn't seem real."

"I know," Beth said, leaning into him slightly. "It's going to be one long day."

Around them, the army of preparers was starting to disperse. Florists made their final adjustments—for now. Gray-and-black-clad security teams compared notes on their datapads, media techs packed up their equipment.

The chapel, which had hummed with activity, began to settle back into its sacred quiet.

CHAPTER
FOURTEEN

THE UNITY CHAPEL echoed with absence. The wedding party had dispersed—Alain to check on his orchids and the various officials to their evening obligations. Even the ever-present security had withdrawn to the perimeter, leaving just the vast space with its soaring columns and ancient stones.

Beth remained in the first pew, staring at her spot on the dais, nodding her head from time to time, muttering the steps of tomorrow's ceremony. The late afternoon light slanted through the high windows, casting her into shadow.

Frankie was on her way behind Spike to the side of the chapel where the media crews had stacked their equipment. Why not use their real-time encrypted connections to call Bruce again. Charge it to Celeste Bellemont.

"Stay?" Beth asked.

Frankie stopped, recognizing the tone—not Distinguished Citizen Blais, not the political performer, just Beth needing to not be alone.

"Of course."

She stepped up to the pew and sat right beside Beth, hip to hip. Spike could make the call on her own.

"Proctor Lizbet would have us running laps for this," Beth said. "Slouching! On sacred architectural elements!"

"Showing insufficient reverence for governmental symbology," Frankie agreed.

They sat in companionable silence for a moment. The hall felt different empty—larger but also more intimate, like a theater after the audience has gone.

"Everyone thinks I'm doing this for duty," Beth said finally. "Even Alain, sometimes. Poor Beth, marrying for politics, sacrificing for the greater good." She laughed, but it wasn't bitter. "They're so busy feeling sorry for me they never ask if I want this."

"Do you?"

"Yes." The word came out firm, certain. "Not the way they think, though. Not because I'm some martyr to tradition or desperate to please the Regent."

Beth picked at a loose thread on her sleeve—the kind of imperfection that would mean a complete outfit change later.

"After Wala, after we were brought here, I spent years trying to earn my place. Perfect grades, perfect behavior, perfect little orphan grateful for rescue." She glanced at Frankie. "We all did, at first. But you figured out faster than the rest of us that we'd never really belong. Not to them."

"Beth—"

"No, you were right. We were trophies. Living proof of Zichi's generosity." Beth's voice stayed steady, almost conversational. "But here's what you missed by leaving—trophies can become real things if you're patient enough."

She stood, walking to the center of the ceremonial circle where tomorrow she'd stand with Alain.

"I'm not marrying into the diCimino family to belong to them.

I'm doing it to change what belonging means." She turned to face Frankie. "Every reform I've pushed through council, every tradition I've 'accidentally' disrupted, every time I've made them include the station kids in planet planning—it all has more weight because I'm on the inside."

"You're infiltrating them with compassion?"

"I'm proving that orphans from tragedy can reshape their precious traditions instead of being shaped by them." Beth's eyes gleamed. "In ten years, twenty, when other girls from the stations or the outer settlements come here, they won't have to perform gratitude. They'll have paths I'm building right now."

Frankie felt her throat tighten. This was the Beth she remembered—the one who'd organized midnight study sessions so everyone could pass, who'd shared her desserts with homesick first-years, who'd always been thinking three moves ahead but with her heart leading the way.

"Plus," Beth added with a grin, "I actually do love Alain. Even if he did compare marriage to a nitrogen cycle during his proposal."

Spike, just to the side of the dais, caught Frankie's eye. She picked up a front paw. Frankie's wristcom buzzed. *Going for a walk.*

Whatever that meant.

"He does seem passionate about soil health," Frankie remembered to say.

"He's very passionate about everything that he really cares about," Beth said. "It's adorable. And useful—do you know how many environmental reforms I've gotten passed while everyone was distracted by his enthusiasm?"

She came back to sit beside Frankie, close enough that their shoulders touched.

Frankie bumped Beth's shoulder gently. "I'm so proud of you."

"And I'm proud of you. Even if I worry every time your friend Bruce mentions you're in 'an interesting situation.'"

"You know Bruce?" Frankie's voice came out sharper than intended.

Beth winced. "I know. Boundaries. But after you went dark for six months that time…"

"I was working."

"You were hiding. There's a difference." Beth's voice gentled. "I don't ask him for details. Just… that you're alive."

Frankie frowned. "You could always ask me."

Beth rolled her eyes. "You never answer your calls."

"Do so!"

"Do not." Beth shook her head, smiling. "Want to know a secret?" she asked suddenly.

"Always."

"I'm glad we're using our sword. The Unity Blade has just the worst motto etched into it. 'Colonization with Care.' Thank Safra they didn't carry on with that motto.

"Well, 'Unity through Order' doesn't seem that much less martial," Frankie said. "More passive-aggressive, I guess."

"I like 'Unity through Understanding,' and not just because of the parallel capitalization."

Frankie laughed. "Good luck with that."

"What?" Beth looked mock affronted. "It's not so impossible. Is it?"

Maybe not for her.

CHAPTER
FIFTEEN

NO OFFICIAL PUBLIC events were scheduled for that evening, thank Safra. Beth was attending a private dinner with her soon-to-be in-laws, all the way down to cousins, and then everyone was supposed to go to bed early.

Or try to find the secret venue where the Screeching Bananas were going to play their 'true fans only' set.

Morgan said he had the address, so he and Celine met Frankie at almost midnight at the main gate to the Regent's Complex. Frankie had to travel in one of the Complex cars, black with big tires and bulletproof doors, but at least it would just drop them off wherever they were going and not linger.

Frankie wore her Bananas concert tunic from the "Banshee" tour, not quite as bright yellow as when she first got it back in university. Nobody needed to know that the actual reason she had it with her was she'd started using it as a sleep shirt. With black tights and her grav boots, she almost looked concert-worthy.

Luckily, Morgan had extra neon glow bracelets and a necklace for her, in the proper Banshee yellow. Celine's were hot pink, while Morgan had made his flashing green necklace into a tiara. Or, hopefully, a headband if he was going to dance.

Not five minutes away from the Complex, Morgan called a stop. The entrance to the old mag-lev tunnels was hidden behind a maintenance panel that he had to pry open with a credit chip. The metal groaned in protest, releasing a gust of stale air that smelled of rust and forgotten decades. Frankie's nose wrinkled—after days of the Complex's perfectly filtered atmosphere, the honest decay was almost refreshing.

"After you," Morgan said with a flourish. They'd turned their neon accessories off, and his dark outfit made him nearly invisible against the tunnel mouth. Smart choice for sneaking around.

Celine descended first, her honey-blonde hair catching the last of the corridor light before they plunged into darkness. Even in the dim emergency lighting, she moved with the same grace she'd shown at every formal event—planet-born confidence in every step. Her tunic and tights were a deep midnight blue that complemented her coloring perfectly, the kind of outfit that said "I can go anywhere and fit in." Next to Morgan's golden features, they looked like they'd been cast by the same designer—matching bookends of privilege and beauty.

The stairs were slick with condensation, and the temperature dropped with each level. The air gained a taste of metal and moisture and something chemical that made her tongue feel funny.

Before they were two levels down, the bass line hit them, vibrating through the concrete and into Frankie's bones. Her teeth ached with it, but in a good way—like finally scratching an itch she hadn't known she had. After days of carefully modulated classical music at formal dinners, the raw power of amplified instruments felt like coming home.

They emerged into a vast convergence where three tunnel mouths met. Hundreds of people had already gathered, their bodies a mass of shadow and movement in the stuttering light of jury-rigged spotlights. The air was thick—sweat and perfume and that underground damp. Someone had brought a fog machine, and the artificial mist mixed with the real moisture to create pockets of opacity that made the space feel infinite and claustrophobic at once.

But the next song was a softie, "You're my second-best friend," just acoustic sitar and voice.

The crowd swayed gently, couples drawing closer, the energy shifting from frenetic to intimate. In the softer atmosphere, Celine's voice carried clearly.

"Second-best friend," she repeated, looking at Morgan. "Is that what I am? Your second-best?"

"You're my number one," Morgan said quickly. "You know that."

Celine's laugh was sharp despite the gentle music. "That's why you orbit stations for a week waiting for Frankie."

Uh-oh.

"We're just friends—" Morgan started.

"Friends?" Celine cut him off. "Friends who wait a week in orbit for each other?"

Frankie felt compelled to intervene. "We really are. Just friends. Morgan needed a ride to—"

"A horse race. Yes, I heard." Celine turned that lawyer's gaze on them both. "If you're 'just friends,' tell me this: Have you ever made love?"

Both Morgan and Frankie winced.

"Thought so," Celine said with grim satisfaction.

"It was just the once," Morgan said quickly.

"And we didn't like it," Frankie added, trying to help.

"We didn't?" Morgan's head whipped toward her, genuine shock on his face.

Frankie rolled her eyes. This was definitely not helping convince Celine of anything.

"I need a drink," Celine announced, her voice cutting through the last notes of the ballad. "Morgan?"

They found a relatively quiet spot near a defunct ticket booth where someone had set up a bar using coolers and determination. The "bartender"—a kid with more piercings than face—handed over three bottles of something that claimed to be beer. Frankie took a sip and nearly coughed. After days of perfectly balanced beverages, the harsh, yeasty rebellion of it shocked her system awake.

"So," Celine said, not touching her bottle. She started to lean against the old tile wall, its checkerboard pattern barely visible under decades of grime, and then thought better of it. "Here we are. Morgan's two favorite people in one convenient location."

"Celine—" Morgan started.

"No, it's fine." She smiled, but Frankie could see the calculation in it—lawyer-in-training weighing her options. "We've been together what, eight months now? Nine if you count that conference on Kestrel where we definitely didn't share a room."

Morgan had the grace to look uncomfortable. Frankie studied her beer bottle's label—apparently "Tunnel Rat Brew" was "brewed with authentic groundwater!"—and tried to become invisible.

"And it's been good," Celine continued. "Really good. You make me laugh, you challenge my assumptions, you look fantastic in formal wear." She gestured at his still-dark outfit. "And whatever that is."

"You know it's more than that," Morgan said softly. He tried to reach for her hand, but she waved him away with a swing of her beer bottle.

Celine turned to Frankie. No hiding now.

"Did you know Morgan proposed? Marriage? To me?"

Frankie couldn't hide her surprise, or her delight. "Fantastic! Weddings must be catching around here."

"She said no," Morgan said, looking away from them, at the tiny raised platform where the band was watching the lead singer and his sitar.

"I did," Celine said. "I found it so interesting that you would rearrange your entire schedule—skip classes, even—to orbit a station for a week. Just waiting." She turned to Frankie. "That's dedication. The kind of dedication I thought we had."

Frankie's stomach clenched. The beer suddenly tasted like guilt.

Celine finally took a sip of her beer, grimacing. "Gods, this is terrible. How do people drink this?"

"With enthusiasm and poor judgment," Morgan said, attempting levity.

"Your two specialties." But Celine's smile was softer now, sadder. "Look, I'm not stupid. I see how you two are together. The little looks, the way you don't even need words half the time. At the formal dinner, you knew she was uncomfortable before she did. I saw it on the feeds."

The music suddenly cut out, the lead singer's voice booming through the tunnels: "Alright, you beautiful underground rebels! Ready to make some noise?"

The crowd roared approval. Frankie felt the sound in her chest cavity, her ribs vibrating with other people's excitement.

"This is 'Gravity Well'—for everyone who's ever been told they don't belong!"

The band exploded into one of their stompers. Morgan's outfit erupted into patterns of light—geometric designs that pulsed with the bass line, shifting from deep purple to electric blue to hot pink. He looked like a walking piece of art, like the music had taken physical form.

"Show off," Celine said, but she was smiling despite herself. She grabbed his newly illuminated hand. "Come on. I hate this band but I love to dance. You too, Frankie. If we're doing this weird triangle thing, might as well move to it."

The crowd was a living organism, bodies moving in chaotic harmony. Frankie let herself be pulled in, feeling the music through the soles of her feet. Everyone seemed to have glow sticks or jewelry like theirs, and they traced neon patterns in the dark. Frankie could taste the fog machine's output—vaguely sweet, probably toxic—and feel the heat rising as hundreds of bodies stomped and danced in the enclosed space.

Celine danced with surprising abandon. But she couldn't shake those formal dance lessons—too much extension, too much precision. Until she finished her beer.

When Celine pressed close to Morgan during a slower section, Frankie could see how well they fit together. Same height, same coloring, same easy comfort with their bodies in space. They looked like what they were: a matched set from the same social stratum.

But Celine still had hold of Frankie's hand.

"You know what your problem is?" Celine said, loud enough for Frankie to hear over the music. "You're in love with the idea of her. The unattainable best friend. It's very romantic, very tragic, very safe."

Morgan's outfit flickered, the patterns stuttering. "That's not—"

"Whereas I'm here. Real. Complicated." She spun, her tunic flaring. "I snore. I eat all the spring rolls at every party. I have opinions about your mother's designs."

"Terrible opinions," Morgan said, but he was smiling.

"Someone has to tell her that not everything needs to glow."

Celine caught Frankie's eye. "What do you think? Should I fight for him? Or is this one of those situations where the childhood friend always wins?"

Before Frankie could form a response that wouldn't make everything worse, the music cut out abruptly. In the sudden silence, her ears rang with phantom bass lines.

Then someone screamed.

Giant shadows erupted across the tunnel walls—massive feline shapes with too many teeth, moving with predatory grace. Frankie's hindbrain screamed *danger* even as her rational mind tried to process what she was seeing. The projections (they had to be projections) seemed to leap from surface to surface, growing larger, more menacing. The fog machine haze made them three-dimensional, solid, real.

The crowd erupted. Bodies slammed into Frankie from all sides as people fled toward the three tunnel exits. Someone knocked over one of the light rigs, sending wild shadows careening across the space. The smell of fear—sharp and animal —cut through everything else. More screams, the crash of equipment, the sound of bottles breaking.

"This way!" Morgan grabbed both their hands, his outfit still pulsing with light, making him a beacon in the chaos.

They pressed against the old ticket booth as the crowd surged past.

Frankie blinked. That shape looked familiar.

She pushed away from Morgan, going against the crowd, heart hammering against her ribs. A elbow caught her in the stomach; someone's drink soaked her shirt. The cold beer against her skin was shocking, grounding.

As the space emptied—even the band—even "Fear Nothing Justin," the lead singer—had vanished—two very real figures emerged from the central tunnel.

Spike padded into the light, her trimmed-sleek fur making her look like a weapon. Every line of her body spoke of controlled power. Beside her, Sterling moved with military precision, his silver coat catching the scattered emergency lights. Both cyvlossics paused at the tunnel mouth, heads tilted, ears swiveling.

Frankie started moving faster, toward the two cyvlossics. Stumbling over shoes, squeeze bulbs of beer, and whatever that gross smell was.

"What the heck?" she said when she reached them.

The cyvlossics surveyed the space with what looked like satisfaction. Equipment lay scattered like aftermath of a battle—abandoned drinks, trampled glow sticks, someone's tunic. Sterling made a sound somewhere between a purr and a growl. Spike responded with a series of chirps that sounded almost like laughter.

They did it on purpose.

They really were cats.

Their shadows—normal-sized now—moved along the walls as they padded further into the space.

Sterling stopped just outside Frankie's reach. His silver eyes fixed on Frankie with unmistakable intensity. He made a series of deliberate movements—head tilting toward the deeper tunnels, then up toward where the wedding venue would be, ears flicking in a pattern that seemed almost like sign language.

Spike padded closer to Frankie, pressing against her leg. The touch looked casual but Frankie felt the tremor of urgency in it.

She bent down. Spike's head turned just enough for her muzzle to brush Frankie's ear.

"Chapel tunnels. Many exits. Must check all." The words were barely more than a breath, steel-on-sandpaper whisper that only Frankie could hear.

"Escape routes?"

"Send the Spear to priority docking." Spike said. "Bruce will pay."

"Okaaay," Frankie said, slow. "We're running away?"

"Extraction may be needed."

The cyvlossics were mapping escape routes from the wedding venue. They must have voted to leave.

"How many?"

"Not all." Spike said. "For now. Negotiating with Bruce. We'll see."

Sterling chirped once—a clear signal—and both cyvlossics turned toward the deeper tunnels. They moved with purpose now, investigation clearly not complete.

Frankie straightened slowly, processing. How was she supposed to get a bunch of well-known not-pets from the tunnels to the orbital station? This plan had holes the size of freighters.

Frankie turned to walk back toward Morgan and Celine. Still huddled by the ticket stand, but looking only a little shaky.

"Were those…?" Celine's voice was very small. Her hand had found Morgan's and gripped tight.

"Did they just…?" Morgan's outfit had gone dark, battery depleted or shocked into silence.

"Clear out a concert with shadow puppets?" Frankie finished. "Yeah. I think they did."

"But why?" Celine asked. She was still holding Morgan's hand, but her brain was clearly spinning.

Now Frankie could hear other voices, other stomps. The cyvlossics weren't the only ones patrolling.

"We should go," she said. "Before security gets here."

They climbed toward the surface in tense silence. Frankie tapped her wristcom to call for the car. She had to call the Spear, tell Ship to come in from the parking cube. Behind them, echoing up from the depths, shouts and signals. The patrol had found their dance floor.

The Complex car was waiting where they'd left it, engine running, ready to return her to her glittering cage. As they climbed in, Frankie couldn't shake the image of those two predators moving through the dark tunnels beneath the city, mapping routes, checking corners, preparing for dangers that only they seemed to fully understand.

And tomorrow was Beth's wedding.

CHAPTER
SIXTEEN

THE DOOR CHIME cut through Frankie's dream like a blade through silk. She'd been somewhere warm, somewhere that smelled like licorice and vanilla—or vanilla licorice? Home, maybe.

Spike launched off the bed before Frankie's eyes were half open, a streak of muscle and attitude heading for the suite's main room. The mattress rocked with her departure, too-soft luxury trying to swallow Frankie back into sleep.

The chime came again. Insistent but not quite emergency-level. Frankie's feet found the cool, soft floor and she stumbled after Spike, rubbing grit from her eyes. The climate control had dropped to nighttime levels, and her second-best sleep shirt did nothing against the chill. Her bare legs prickled with goosebumps.

"Who visits at—" She picked up her wristcom. "Two in the morning?" They'd only got back from the Screaming Bananas concert debacle an hour ago.

Spike was already at the door, nose pressed to the crack at the bottom, making small interrogative noises. Not growling, which meant not a threat. Just someone who shouldn't be here.

Frankie palmed the door control, ready to be irritated at whatever Capital nonsense—

Beth tumbled in like she'd been leaning against the door. She caught herself with one hand on the frame, the other clutching… something. Frankie's sleep-foggy brain took a moment to process the visual.

Beth wore sleep pants, soft and Cooperative gray, with a formal reception tunic thrown over them, crystal beading at the scoop neck catching the low light. No shoes, toenails painted the precise shade of "understated power." Her perfect hair was hidden under a lumpy kerchief, probably bound six ways to Sunday for whatever astounding style she'd planned for tomorrow.

Today.

"I can't—" Beth's words came out in a rush, tumbling over each other like scattered pearls. "I was in bed and then I remembered the seating charts need approval but that's not—it doesn't matter because tomorrow I'm getting married and someone said —at the reception tonight someone said I'll make an excellent Regent someday and I wanted to scream but instead I smiled and said thank you like that's a compliment and not a curse and—"

Frankie caught her friend's shoulders, felt the tremor running through her like a low-frequency hum. Spike pushed the door shut.

"I can't breathe!" But Beth did, one shuddering inhale. Frankie slid an arm down Beth's side, pulling them close at the hip. She smelled like berries and worry.

"I can't breathe because I'm turning into her. Into all of them. I give orders and people jump. I smile and legislation passes. I'm not even thirty-five and I'm already a institution instead of a person. And Alain—"

Her voice cracked on her fiancé's name. The thing in her hand revealed itself to be a shoe, a satiny number with matching heel. Fancy dinner shoe, or go to chapel shoe. She looked at it like she'd never seen footwear before, and then dropped it on the floor.

"I was almost asleep and I found myself rehearsing tomorrow's schedule in thirty-second intervals. Thirty seconds, Freddie! Frankie, sorry. For my own wedding! When did I become someone who schedules joy?"

Spike wound around Beth's ankles, a move that would have been comforting from a normal cat but looked vaguely threatening from a half-meter-tall cyvlossic. Beth didn't seem to notice.

Frankie tugged her toward the bedroom. "If we're going to have a panic attack at least have it somewhere comfortable."

Beth let herself be led, words still spilling out in choppy bursts. "The flowers are wrong. Not wrong, perfect. Too perfect. Everything's too perfect. I wanted wildflowers, you know, like a hillside wedding. But wildflowers aren't appropriate for a state wedding and everything's inside, so now I have white bluebells that smell like I can't even remember what and—"

"Bluebells smell?" Frankie guided Beth to sit on the bed's edge.

"These ones do. Alain engineered them specially. They're not really bluebells; they're an offshoot. They smell like…"

Beth paused, blinking. "Actually they smell lovely. Like vanilla and rain. Why am I angry about flowers that smell like rain?"

"Because you're getting married in the morning." Frankie sat beside her, the mattress dipping to push their shoulders together. Beth was nice and warm. Overheated. "Which would freak anyone out. And when you're freaked out, you get mean about details."

"I do not get mean."

Spike jumped onto the foot of the bed with a grunt. She settled into a circle, lay her head down, and was asleep instantly. Crawling the train tunnels with Sterling must have taken it out of her.

"Beth. You made a proctor cry over napkin angles when you took your advanced etiquette practical."

"The angles were mathematically inconsistent!" But Beth was starting to sound more like herself. The tremor eased, though her hands still clutched each other painfully. "Oh, Frankie, I can't marry him."

"Why not?"

"Because I'm … hollow." The words came out small, fragile as spun glass. "I'm very good at seeming full—full of purpose and passion and all the things real people have. But inside I'm just… protocols and performance. What happens when he figures that out?"

Frankie studied her friend in the dim light. Even in disaster, Beth maintained a certain dignity—spine straight despite the mismatched clothing, chin up despite the tears threatening to spill. The formal tunic's beading caught the light with each breath.

"You know what I did today?" Beth continued, staring at her bare feet. "I solved a three-system water rights dispute. Sixty years of conflict, resolved over lunch. And the whole time I was thinking about whether my wedding favors convey the appropriate level of gratitude without seeming clingy."

"Did you solve it well? The water thing?"

Beth blinked. "Yes? Three colonies will have sustainable access, and the mining consortium gets regulated usage that won't deplete—why does that matter?"

"Because a hollow person wouldn't care if three colonies had water." Frankie bumped her shoulder against Beth's. "They'd only care about the political points."

"I do care about the political points."

"Sure. But you care about the water, too." Frankie scooted to the head of the bed, arranging the obscene number of pillows so she could sit up. She pulled Beth by the hand to sit next to her. She tucked their legs under the still-warm duvet.

Beth picked up one of the square pillows and hugged it to her. She leaned the back of her head against the wall and closed her wounded eyes. "When did you get wise?"

"Tuesdays and alternate Thursdays."

"But never on Mondays," Beth finished the lyric.

"You're a secret Screeching Bananas fan!" Frankie gave Beth's shoulder the softest punch. "We saw them tonight. They were playing that song when we got there."

"Still great?"

"So great." Frankie sighed, wishing the show had gone longer. Wishing Celine hadn't come. "It was in the abandoned transit tunnels. I got beer all over me—and it wasn't even my beer!"

"Sounds perfect."

"Don't patronize," Frankie said. "We can't all love diplomatic legalese. So. Do you love him?"

"Alain?" Beth's face softened. "He doesn't see a Distinguished Citizen when he looks at me." Beth's voice dropped to a whisper. "He sees someone who might want to hear about nitrogen cycles. Or just cuddle and not talk at all. Do you know how rare that is?"

"Sounds perfect." For her.

A watery laugh escaped. "I'm going to marry a man who follows his passions, damn the consequences. Willing to listen to me work out a complicated negotiation day after day after day. Or pretend to, anyway."

"I think he listens."

Beth grabbed Frankie's hand, tight. "What if I ruin him? What if I take this sweet, brilliant man who gets emotional about tomatoes and turn him into another Capital chess piece?"

The air filters hummed, filling the silence while Frankie searched for words. The bed was too big, the suite felt too big around them. All that empty space pressing in. Bigger than the main floor of their house on Wala. The thought came unbidden, bringing with it the usual complicated knot of survivor's guilt and gratitude and anger at having to be grateful.

"Remember when we were fourteen," Frankie said finally, "and you organized that study group for the local scholarship kids?"

"That was basic peer tutoring—"

"You called it that. But really you were teaching kids from the outer settlements how to navigate Capital exams without losing themselves. You made sure everyone knew the tricks while keeping their own ways of thinking." Frankie set her other hand over their clasped ones, and squeezed them. "You've always been someone who helps people stay themselves while succeeding. Why would you stop now?"

Beth squeezed back, her grip almost painful. "Because the higher you rise, the less room there is to be yourself. And I'm so high now I can barely see who I started as."

"I can see her." Frankie's throat felt tight. "She's right here. Wearing a masterpiece of beading over her pajamas and worrying herself to death about someone else."

That startled a real laugh out of Beth. "This tunic is a museum piece, actually."

"And you threw it over your sleep clothes to run through the halls at two in the morning. The Beth who follows protocol wouldn't have done that."

"The Beth who follows protocol would have scheduled her breakdown for daylight hours." But she was smiling now, tears finally spilling over but not seeming quite so desperate. "With forms signed by three neutral observers."

Spike made a rumbling sound that might have been agreement or just digestion. The cyvlossic had sprawled across the foot of the bed, taking up more space than physics should allow.

"I haven't slept in two days," Beth admitted. "Every time I close my eyes, I see seating charts. Do you know how many ways you can arrange four hundred people to either prevent or cause diplomatic incidents?"

"Too many?"

"Factorial four hundred. It's a number so large it stops having meaning." She leaned into Frankie's shoulder. "I had someone run probability scenarios."

"Of course you did."

"There's a twelve percent chance of at least one major incident regardless of arrangement. Fifteen percent if the Okoye delegation drinks."

"They always drink."

"I know!" Beth's voice pitched higher. "And I can't serve okeye at my own wedding, but Ambassador Okoye gets handsy after three glasses of anything real, and her wife carries a ceremonial knife that's technically functional, and—"

"Beth."

"—the Bellemont family can't sit near any media equipment or they'll turn my wedding into content, but they're major donors so they can't be back-row, and—"

"Beth."

"—my old roommate from the outer colonies uses the wrong fork on purpose to make points about classism, which I respect but not at my wedding, and—"

"Beth!" Frankie grabbed her friend's face between her palms, forcing eye contact. "Do you want to marry Alain?"

Beth blinked. "Yes."

"Then everything else is just noise."

"It's very loud noise. With diplomatic consequences."

"So let them have consequences. Let Okoye get drunk. Let

your cousin use a soup spoon for the fish course. Let the Bellemont family turn it into a reality show." Frankie released Beth's face but held her gaze. "The worst thing that happens is you have an interesting wedding instead of a perfect one."

"The Regent—"

"Has seen it all. Will handle what needs handling. That's literally her job." Frankie felt certainty settling into her bones. "Your job is to marry the man who thinks soil pH is pillow talk."

Frankie pulled her friend sideways until they were both lying on the enormous bed, staring at the ceiling. The fabric above was midnight blue, scattered with tiny lights meant to mimic stars. Unexpected illusion, but comforting.

Spike grumbled at the disruption but adjusted. Prima donna —their feet didn't even come near the cyvlossic.

"I can't go back to my room," Beth said to the fake stars. "My staff will be there at five to start preparations. If they find me like this…"

"So stay." The words came easy as breathing. "Here, I'll set an alarm. You can sneak back at four-thirty like we're still teenagers breaking curfew."

"We never broke curfew."

"You never broke curfew." Frankie found Beth's hand again in the darkness. "You're braver now."

They lay in silence, breathing falling into sync the way it had in dormitory beds years ago. Frankie pulled the covers over both of them, formal tunic and sleep clothes and all.

SEVENTEEN

THE NOTE WAS WAITING, tucked under Frankie's door in the blue hour before dawn—a thick, creamy rectangle of real paper, the kind pressed by hand, the kind you kept forever. She found it with the ball of her foot, nearly skidding on its unexpected friction. Her heart thudded, instantly awake.

My dear Francesca, Please join me for tea at first light. The small study. Come as you are

—E

E. Not "Eurydice diCimino, Regent of the Cooperative Realm." Not the formal seal that turned invitations into commands. Just E, written in handwriting that showed the faintest tremor. Age or emotion? Both?

Frankie stared at it, thumb running over the fibers. She'd been summoned to the small study three times as a child. Once after a diplomatic incident involving a soup spoon and a visiting senator. Once after she'd gone missing for an afternoon and been found hiding in the city library. And once—she remembered this most clearly—after she'd locked herself in a storage closet for three hours to avoid being paraded at yet another "inspirational orphan" event

Each time, it had been a reckoning. Each time, her body had remembered the shape of dread: heartbeat in her throat, stiff knees, the taste of old fear rising like acid.

She looked toward the window out to the garden. Was it almost dawn? Whatever, she couldn't sleep anyways.

She could refuse. She was an adult now, Ship's captain, a person with choices. But Beth's wedding was today, and Frankie was curious.

And "come as you are" was absolute bullshit. Frankie changed into a tunic that was both formal and soft, the one Beth had picked out for "civilized emergencies." Matching wide blue pants, gold embroidery, no jewelry. She left her wristcom behind, as was the rule.

The corridors were different at dawn. Nearly empty, muffled by the thick hush that hung over the Complex in the early morning. The air tasted of distant flowers and something older—that green polish that somehow never made the floors turn green.

Her slipper-shoes made no sound on the cold marble as she ghosted past the formal rooms and into the halls marked with red lights along the floor's edge. Her pulse, on the other hand, was a drumbeat.

Proctor Merin, all in gray, was waiting for her as she turned the corner just past the Regent's Library and into a narrow hallway. Her posture as upright as ever, her expression unreadable, and even at this hour, her hair was an architecture of severity.

It felt like stepping backward through time. The ceiling lowered here, the walls shifted from marble to warm wood that released a scent of polish and age. As she followed the proctor, Frankie's fingers trailed along the paneling, finding the tiny dents and scratches that expensive restoration had carefully preserved. History, curated and contained.

The old-fashioned wood door was ajar, spilling butter-yellow light into the dim corridor. Frankie heard the soft clink of porcelain, the whisper of liquid being poured. No servants' footsteps. Her shoulders tensed automatically, muscle memory of a twelve-year-old trying to make herself smaller, less noticeable, less of a disappointment.

Proctor Merin knocked, two short raps that sounded too loud in the morning hush.

"Come."

The voice was smaller than Frankie remembered. Less resonant. Just an old woman's voice, really, without the amplification of authority.

Merin waved Frankie forward. Frankie pushed the door open and stopped, her breath catching like fabric on a rough edge.

The room was nothing like her terror-memories had painted it. Sure, the bones were the same—the built-in old-fashioned book shelves, the window overlooking the kitchen gardens, the chairs arranged for intimate conversation. But now she could see what child-eyes had missed.

The air was thick with the scent of old paper, chamomile, and something sweet and unfamiliar. A worn rattan rug, its edges curling, covering most of the floor. A quilt draped over the reading chair, handmade with slightly crooked stitches. On one wall, children's drawings hung in cheap, mismatched frames—Frankie recognized one, a lopsided spaceship under a green sun, her own signature a blue scrawl in the corner.

And the Regent herself. Smaller than Frankie remembered, sipping tea from a fragile porcelain bowl at a small round wooden table by the window. No formal robes, no power-dressed severity. Just a woman in a simple morning dress the color of old pearls, her silver hair down, exposing the soft vulnerability of her neck.

For a moment, neither of them moved. Frankie's vision flickered: she was twelve again, all bones and wild hair, summoned for judgment; she was thirty-two, a pilot, a survivor, a woman who could choose to walk away. She hovered in the doorway, every muscle braced.

"Francesca. Fridrika." The Regent shook her head. "I can't believe we changed your names." She sighed, and waved a hand toward the wingback chair that matched her own. "Thank you for coming."

No titles. No "Citizen Styles." Just her name, and not the one the Complex had given her. Something in Frankie's chest softened, the tiniest bit.

She took a step in. And another.

The Regent gestured to the armchair opposite, its seat worn to a shine. The table between them was crowded with mismatched mugs, a battered teapot, a plate of honey biscuits.

"How do you take your tea?"

"Black," Frankie lied automatically, the way she always did when someone might judge her preferences.

"Hmm." The Regent's mouth quirked, almost a smile. "You used to drown it in honey when you thought no one was looking. The kitchen staff found it endearing."

Heat crawled up Frankie's neck. Even her preferences had been monitored, catalogued, found acceptable or wanting. She sat carefully, the chair accepting her weight with a soft sigh.

"I wanted to see you without the performance," the Regent said, pouring tea with hands that shook just slightly. "Both yours and mine."

The tea was too hot, scorching Frankie's fingers as she held the bowl, and her tongue when she sipped to avoid responding. It tasted of earth and flowers and something a little bitter.

A silence grew between them, thick as the honey the Regent spooned into her own cup. Outside, a bird called. The old floor creaked as the building settled. Frankie's heart slowed, her hands unclenching by degrees.

"You look well," the Regent continued. "Better than at dinner. Morning light suits you more than chandeliers."

Was that a compliment or criticism? Frankie couldn't parse it, couldn't find the trap in the words. The morning light in question, artificial yet lovely, slanted through the window, painting geometric patterns on the worn carpet. Dust motes danced in the beams like tiny planets, and Frankie found herself watching them to avoid the Regent's soft yet too-sharp eyes.

"Four of you." The words came soft as moth wings. "All of Wala, just you four. I think about that more than you might imagine."

Frankie's hand stilled on her teacup. The porcelain was rough beneath her fingers, someone's earnest attempt at beauty that hadn't quite succeeded. Like all of them, maybe. Attempts at remaking that never quite took.

"I wanted to see you," the Regent said at last, her voice rough. "Not as a Regent. Not as a symbol. Not as an obligation. Just as myself. And yourself, if you can bear it."

Frankie set her mug down, the click louder than she expected. Her voice, when it came, was raw. "Why now?"

The Regent's lips twisted, half smile, half wince. "Because I am old enough now to know that regret is heavier than any crown. And because you are leaving again, and I may not get another chance." She looked down at her hands, tracing the lines of her knuckles. "I am not good at apologies. I was trained to command, to endure, to survive. I have been a poor mother to this house, and a poorer one to you."

Frankie stared at the old woman, seeing for the first time the cost of all that survival. The lines around her mouth, the deep shadows under her eyes. The way her hands shook as she reached for the teapot.

The Regent continued, voice gathering strength. "We told ourselves we were rescuing you. We told ourselves you should be grateful. But what we really did was put you in a new kind of cage, one lined with velvet and good intentions. I let them change your name, thinking it would help you fit in. I let them parade you for the cameras, thinking it would help you belong. I let you believe you had to earn your place here—by being good, by being useful, by being silent."

Frankie's vision blurred. She gripped the arms of the chair, fighting the urge to vanish into the woodwork. "I was grateful," she whispered. "I was safe."

The Regent shook her head, her voice breaking. "Safety is not the same as love. I see that now. You were a child, grieving, and I asked you to perform gratitude instead of letting you mourn."

A silence fell, deeper than before. Frankie felt the ache of old wounds, the ghost of a thousand staged smiles. She remembered the cold glare of camera drones, the weight of formal robes, the ache of holding herself still.

The Regent reached into a tiny drawer inset into the underside of the table—real wood, it creaked slightly—and withdrew a paper photograph. Not The Photograph, the one that haunted newscasts and memorial services, but another. She held it out, her hand trembling.

Frankie at twelve, three years into her Complex residency. The photographer had caught her trying to smile, but her eyes gave away everything—the haunted wariness, the desperate desire to be good enough, the exhaustion of performance already settling into her small bones. She wore the regulation gray-and-yellow tunic that never fit quite right, despite all the proctor's attempts at tailoring. Behind her, the common room looked vast and cold despite its warm colors.

"I keep this near," the Regent said, soft, "to remind myself of what I lost. What I took from you. I look at it every day, and I ask forgiveness from the girl in the photograph."

Frankie traced her own face with a fingertip, feeling a lump rise in her throat. "I don't know if I can," she said, her voice a thread.

The Regent nodded, a single, grave motion. "You tried so hard to be grateful," she said. "It broke my heart then. It still does."

The words stole Frankie's breath. She could taste that desperation suddenly, metallic and sharp—the flavor of trying to earn safety, of performing gratitude like a trained animal for the reward of belonging.

Frankie looked up, meeting the Regent's gaze for the first time. The old woman's eyes glistened, but she held Frankie's gaze, unflinching.

A bird called in the garden outside, its morning song bright and oblivious. The sound was so normal, so disconnected from this conversation, that Frankie felt slightly unmoored. How could birds sing while old wounds opened like flowers?

The Regent reached across the small table, her hand hovering near Frankie's but not quite touching. The space between them felt charged, full of possibility and old pain. Frankie could see the veins through the aged skin, blue rivers mapping a long life. Could smell the faint scent of expensive lotion, lavender and something medicinal.

"You were a child when your planet was erased, may all rest in peace," she said. "I was a baby Regent, not one year into this role. I'd never had to face such a devastation before. No one had. I'd lost an entire planet, during my watch. I thought I should resign, just quit."

Frankie, shocked, set her hand on top of the Regent's cool one.

"I couldn't, of course. Lucien wasn't even twelve, and the Families were restive." She set her tea saucer down, and set her other hand on Frankie's. "But I didn't handle everything well. I let you believe you needed to earn your place here, when of course you deserved safety and care simply because you were a child who needed it."

"I wish I had thought first of you, instead of appearances. I wish I had called you Fridrika every day, instead of Francesca. I wish I hadn't been a brand-new regent when this disaster happened."

Frankie's eyes burned suddenly, viciously. She blinked hard, refusing the tears. The twelve-year-old who'd needed those words was gone, wasn't she? But her ghost sat heavy in Frankie's chest, aching with want.

Sunlight crept across the rattan flooring. Frankie could feel through her slippers, a gentle heat that made her aware of her own body, her own presence in this space that had once made her feel like nothing.

"When Beth told me you were coming," the Regent continued, "she was terrified. I could see it. Not of the wedding going wrong. Of you seeing who she's become. She thinks she's betrayed you somehow by thriving here."

Frankie's breath came shaky, her voice a whisper. "Beth saved me."

The Regent smiled, her tears shining in the morning light. "You saved each other."

"Beth needs you at this wedding," the Regent continued, her hands withdrawing to wrap around her cooling tea. "But more importantly, afterwords. She needs someone who knew her before she became what we helped make her. Someone who sees Bethie, not Distinguished Citizen Blais."

A laugh escaped Frankie, sharp and surprised. It tasted like bitter chocolate, dark and complex. "I can't stay."

"No." Simple acknowledgment, no deflection. "But you might call more."

The Regent leaned back, and picked up her tea.

Outside, more birds joined the first, creating a cacophony of daily joy. The kitchen gardens released their scents to the warming air—basil and rosemary and something sweet Frankie couldn't identify.

Frankie studied the Regent as she gazed out the window, seeing past the authority to the woman beneath. There were lines around her eyes from squinting, from smiling, from carrying the weight of too many decisions. Without her traditional black lipstick, her mouth was pale and somehow more honest.

The birds chirped on, oblivious. The gardens released their perfume.

Frankie stood slowly. Her legs felt weak, but her heart was lighter, somehow, as if some ancient weight had shifted.

"May I make a copy of this?" she asked, holding up the photograph.

"Keep it," the Regent said, her voice thick. "It belongs to you."

Frankie slipped it into her pocket, the edges pressing against her hip like a promise.

CHAPTER
EIGHTEEN

THE CHAMBER of Composure hummed with a frequency that made Frankie's teeth ache. Two levels beneath the Unity Chapel, carved from the same ancient rock that anchored the memorial garden a kilometer to the east, the crystal-lined room seemed to breathe with its own rhythm. The walls shifted color with each pulse—currently a nervous orange that flickered toward red whenever someone moved too quickly.

Frankie, already dolled up in the Cooperatives' image of Walan finery, sat cross-legged on a stone bench, staring at the collection of objects before her: a vial of oil that smelled like sour cherries, three light-fibers that writhed like luminous worms, and a chunk of crystal that was either very important or someone's idea of a joke. Around her, eleven other women moved through preparations with practiced grace, each attending to Beth with the confidence of people who'd done this before.

They hadn't, of course. The last Regent's wedding was almost two generations ago. But they moved as if guided by genetic memory, as if their noble blood carried the instructions Frankie's orphan genes lacked. Or a righteous fear of the Protocol Minister.

"The oil must be applied counter-clockwise," Lindy Chen-Okoye instructed, her fingers tracing spirals on Beth's left temple. "For fertility and fortune."

"Clockwise," corrected Anna Varga from the Hargan delegation. "Unless you want her children born backwards."

"That's superstition," sniffed someone else—Frankie had lost track of names and families. "The direction matters only for the light-fiber activation."

Beth stood at the center of it all, still as a statue while hands moved around her, through her hair, across her skin. The formal undergown—if you could call the geometric web of metallic fabric a gown—left her arms and shoulders bare for the ritual markings. Temporary tattoos from three different worlds created a map of political alliance on her skin, visible only under certain spectrums of light. During the ceremony, she would literally glow with cooperation.

Frankie picked up one of her light-fibers. It squirmed away from her touch, maybe seeking something with more electrical potential. Around her, the other women wove their fibers into Beth's hair with expert motions, creating a crown of living light that would pulse with her biorhythms during the ceremony. Frankie's fiber did nothing but writhe.

"You have to think at it," suggested Cindy Morrison, the youngest at fourteen. "They respond to focused intention."

Frankie thought at it. The fiber tied itself into a knot.

"Perhaps..." Cindy reached for the fiber, then pulled back. "No, you should do it. The blessing is more powerful from a heart-sister."

Heart-sister. The Walan term for non-relatives raised together. What a strange detail for a youngster to remember.

The chamber's hum shifted, a half-tone higher. The walls flashed yellow—someone's emotional spike disrupting the harmony. Through the part of the translucent floor that wasn't covered by the square patch of royal purple Beth was standing on, Frankie could see movement in the kitchen and prep level below, dark shapes against the utilitarian lighting. Those early citizens of Zichi must have been master diggers.

"Five minutes for the Moment of Solitary Reflection," announced Anna Varga. "We'll apply the final layer after."

The others filed out through the chamber's iris door, their ceremonial robes creating a whisper of expensive fabric and subtle perfume. The door sealed, and the walls shifted to a deep blue, leaving just Frankie and Beth in the humming silence.

Beth's eyes snapped open. "I can't breathe."

"It's the oils. Why so many? Here—" Frankie grabbed a ceremonial cloth and dabbed at Beth's temples. "Better?"

"The smells are fighting each other. And these things—" Beth gestured at the light-fibers in her hair, which had synchronized into a slow, hypnotic wave. "They're moving. I can feel them moving."

"That's probably normal?"

"Nothing about this is normal." Beth's laugh had an edge of hysteria. "Look at this undergown. I'm wearing a mathematical equation. Lindy says it represents the unified field theory."

"Well, you do look very… theoretical."

That got a real laugh. Beth reached out and grabbed Frankie's oil-stained hand. "At least it's comfortable. What if I drop it?"

It took a moment to figure out drop what. "The blade?"

"In front of everyone. In front of the entire Cooperative. What if it rejects me like it did the test subjects? What if—" Her voice dropped. "What if it knows I don't belong up there?"

Frankie squeezed back, remembering. "It knew you yesterday, remember? Every single time. How many did the minister make you do?"

"A dozen times, at least." Beth sighed. She lifted her hands to run them through her hair, and then thought better of it.

The chamber hummed higher, walls shifting toward green. Through the floor, a couple of cyvlossics in the kitchen seemed to be having some kind of meeting. Weird.

"Are cyvlossics allowed in the kitchen?" Beth asked, following her gaze. "Why aren't they with their people?"

Why, indeed.

The iris door dilated. Anna Varga swept in, carrying the final ceremonial layer—a blue-black sheath that seemed to be made of condensed starlight. "Time, ladies. The chapel awaits."

The other women flooded back, surrounding Beth with practiced efficiency. The light-fibers in her hair responded to something in the dress, creating a halo effect that made her look otherworldly. The temporary tattoos began to emerge as the chamber's lighting shifted, turning her skin into a living treaty document.

"Citizen Styles," Lindy Morrison said. "You'll carry the train." She handed Frankie some silver fabric rolled into a log, and then pulled the edge and fastened two corners to the shoulders of Beth's dress. "It's reactive fabric—try to keep your emotional state neutral, or it will display your feelings in color."

Fantastic.

They formed a line, Beth at the center, Frankie immediately behind. The chamber's hum reached a crescendo, and the walls flashed through a rainbow sequence. The signal to ascend.

The spiral passage wound upward through the rock. Frankie's inner ear protested, but she focused on the train in her hands. The fabric rippled with Beth's emotions—gold confidence shifting to silver anxiety and back again. Before and behind them, the other women began a low chant, the sounds bouncing off the stone walls in eerie harmonics.

Light increased as they climbed. Natural light, not the chamber's artificial glow. The murmur of hundreds of voices grew louder—the chapel filling with witnesses. Through ventilation slots, Frankie caught glimpses of the main space. The morning sun through the stained glass created patterns that seemed to move with their own intelligence.

They emerged behind a white fabric screen hiding them from what sounded like a maelstrom.

"The Hargan delegation needs to move back three rows—their climate fields are interfering with the Okoye sensors!"

"Someone tell Senator Voss that her cyvlossic cannot sit IN the pew!"

"There's a media drone tangled in the vine of the room. Again!"

The Protocol Minister stood at the center of it all, datapad in one hand, ceremonial staff in the other, looking like she might use either as a weapon. Her two gray-clad assistants scurried about, handling wound-up guests, while security personnel tried to herd calmer ones into proper positions.

"No, no, NO!" The protocol minister's voice cut through the noise. "The Newer Territories delegation sits on the left, behind the Chen-Okoyes, not in front of them! Do you want to start an interplanetary incident?"

A senior diplomat was helped to a different row, muttering in his clicking language what were probably profanities.

"Where do the late arrivals from Epsilon station go?" An assistant held a datapad like a shield.

"Section G, rows 4 through 6. And remind them that recording devices are strictly prohibited during the harmonic tuning—last time someone's device created a feedback loop that shattered three windows."

The women helped Beth into the preparation alcove—a small chamber to the side of the main chapel where she would wait for her entrance. The others dispersed to their seats, leaving Frankie and Beth with a moment of relative quiet.

"Sounds like we're off schedule already," Frankie said,

unrolling Beth's train. Not one wrinkle. "So much for those thirty-second increments."

"This is actually going smoothly," Beth said. "At the Nguyen-Castillo wedding, two delegations claimed the same seats and had to solve it with a formal debate that took three hours."

Through the alcove's one-way window, they could watch the seating drama unfold. Morgan, hair tamed and in sober burgundy, was trying to squeeze into a row that was clearly full, his long legs creating a traffic jam. Celina, five rows back with a space beside her, could not seem to catch his attention. David sat rigid in the third row, tapping his datapad obsessively. First Citizen Bellemont held court near the center, her cyvlossic Prism color-shifting nervously at her feet.

"The Morrison delegation's climate field is conflicting with the air recyclers!" someone shouted.

"Turn it down to 15 percent!"

"But Lady Morrison has a respiratory condition!"

"Move them to Section F! Say the ventilation is better there!"

More shuffling. More muttered complaints. One of the media drones that had gotten stuck in a flower arrangement was now trailing purple petals as it tried to escape.

"Remember," Frankie said, squeezing Beth's hand. "You've got a grip like magnets."

"Like magnets," Beth repeated, but her train had gone a worried purple. She noticed Frankie staring at it and took a deep breath. The train eased into puce.

A hand signal from the protocol minister—Frankie needed to take her seat. She gave Beth a quick kiss on the cheek—not marring the face powder. "Knock 'em dead."

Beth choke-laughed. "Don't even say that."

Frankie made her way to the Peripheral Gallery, left side, row seven, inner aisle. The older woman beside her leaned over, smelling of roses and talc. "First time?"

"Yes."

"Oh, you're in for a treat. Though nothing compared to the ones before the war. Did you know they used to release live butterflies? Had to stop when the Hargans showed up. They're allergic."

Around them, the final seating adjustments were being made. A young couple was forcibly separated—apparently unmarried pairs couldn't sit together in Section B. Someone's companion robot was politely but firmly told to wait outside. The Voss delegation's temperature requirements had created a microclimate that was fogging up the reporter's video glasses in their section.

"Citizens and Delegates," the protocol minister's voice rang out, somehow both private and everywhere at once. The chapel's acoustics carried it to every corner without amplification. "We begin with the Harmonic Tuning. Please, find your note."

An ancient instrument—something between a bell and a singing bowl—released a single, pure tone. The congregation was meant to match it, creating a unified resonance that would literally tune the chapel's crystalline components.

Around her, hundreds of voices rose, joining Frankie's, seeking harmony. The Hargan delegates found it first, their voices blending into something that made the wall near them sing back. The children's choir joined, adding harmonics that turned the simple tone into something complex. Others followed, each world adding its own flavor to the sound.

Frankie hummed, hoping she was close. Beside her, the older woman's voice was surprisingly strong and perfectly pitched. Two rows ahead, a tone-deaf diplomat from the Newer Territories was actively sabotaging the entire left section. The protocol minister's expression suggested murder might be traditional after all.

"Sharp!" someone hissed. "You're sharp!"

"I'm doing my best!" the diplomat protested.

Three long minutes later, they achieved something

approaching harmony. The sound made all the chapel's walls resonate. The stained glass rang in frequencies that painted new colors in the air. The sound swelled, creating a moment of perfect unity.

Then someone's device did create feedback, and a small window in the back shattered. She wondered if it was David's.

"Every time," the woman next to Frankie sighed. "There's always one."

The light paths activated.

Frankie had heard about this but never seen it. The purple carpet began to glow from within, bio-reactive elements responding to the harmonic frequency. The main doors opened with theatrical slowness.

The congregation rose as one, the movement creating a wave of light in the reactive flooring.

The Regent entered first. She wore a flowing tunic of deep gold that fell to her knees, its fabric seeming to hold light within its weave. The tunic's long sleeves were close-fitted to the elbow before opening into graceful bells, each edge traced with purple thread so fine it looked painted on. Beneath, matching trousers in a lighter tan silk narrowed at the ankles, allowing glimpses of ceremonial slippers that clicked authority with each step.

Her diadem was deceptively simple—a band of gold that sat low on her forehead, widening slightly at the center where a single purple stone rested. No ostentatious height, no frivolous decoration. Just power, worn lightly.

The tunic's embroidery told stories in abstract patterns—interlocking spirals and angular knots that suggested ancient treaties, the binding of worlds, the weight of promises kept and broken. The designs seemed to shift in the light, revealing different meanings from different angles. Around the hem and neckline, the purple thread formed protective wards that looked almost runic, as if she wore the mathematical equations of peace itself.

Her footsteps triggered cascades of light in the floor, purple energy flowing outward from each contact. But the color shifted with each step—deep blue confidence, gold satisfaction, a flicker of orange when she noticed Sterling sitting at Senator Voss's feet instead of his assigned position. The congregation rose again, the movement creating another wave in the reactive flooring.

She walked the length of the chapel, her emotional state written in light for all to see. By the time she reached her protected box, the purple had settled into a steady royal blue. Watchful. Ready.

"She's nervous about something," the older woman whispered. "That blue is too steady. She's controlling it."

Lucien followed twelve steps behind. His high-collared jacket was such a deep burgundy that it made the usual shade of succession red seem almost crude by comparison. A military cut, gold piping traced every edge from shoulder to calf with geometric precision. The white ceremonial sash across his chest caught the light like liquid metal, marking him as heir without overwhelming his role as brother. Everything about him was controlled, from the mirror-shine boots to the decorative blade at his hip that somehow managed to look both ceremonial and genuinely lethal.

Where Alain would soon appear in flowing fabrics that moved like plants in the wind, Lucien was all sharp angles. He moved like a soldier playing at ceremony, each gesture precise but somehow grudging, as if formal weddings were just another type of battlefield requiring different tactics.

His light path along the carpet briefly intersected with his mother's, creating interference patterns where they crossed. His colors were more volatile—green anxiety spiking to red irritation when someone's camera drone got too close. But training won. By the time he reached the front, his footsteps glowed steady amber. Determination tinged with what might have been resignation.

"Poor boy," Frankie's companion murmured. "The weight of succession. My nephew went through the same thing back on Garland Two. Started losing his hair at thirty."

A pause. The protocol minister, standing just below the dais, raised her staff.

From the eastern entrance, Alain stepped into the Pool of Reflection. His feet were bare, as tradition demanded, and each step through the shallow water left glowing prints on the stone beyond. Bioluminescent organisms clung to his skin, creating an effect like walking starlight. His path would spiral around the chapel's edge, collecting blessings from each delegation.

"Oh!" the older woman gasped. "He's using Vintage Aurora strain. Those haven't been seen in fifty years. How did he—of course, he's a botanist, isn't he?"

From the western entrance, Beth appeared.

The congregation's collective intake of breath was a thunderclap. The light-fibers in her hair had synchronized with her heartbeat, creating a crown of pulsing radiance. The temporary tattoos glowed through the translucent ceremony gown, turning her into a living document of unity. Her own water-light footprints began their spiral, moving opposite to Alain's.

"Beautiful," Frankie's neighbor whispered.

"The dress is Nguyen design," another voice added. "See the equations in the weave?"

They would meet at the dais, their paths creating a double helix of light around the congregation.

Frankie watched Beth move with trained grace, pausing at each delegation for the ritual touch of blessing. The Hargan ambassador pressed two fingers to Beth's forehead. The Smithson representative traced a symbol on her palm. Each contact left a brief glow on her skin, another layer of ceremonial significance.

At the Morrison delegation, Lady Morrison's respiratory condition chose that moment to act up. Her coughing fit disrupted Beth's rhythm, but Beth smoothly incorporated it, holding the lady's hand until the spasms passed. The gesture turned what could have been embarrassing into a moment of compassion.

Alain, meanwhile, had stopped to examine the flower arrangements. Even in ceremony, he couldn't resist. His fingers traced the edge of a particularly rare bloom, and his footprints veered off the prescribed path.

"Distinguished Citizen," the protocol minister hissed, just loud enough for the acoustics to catch.

Alain jumped, his bio-luminescent trail flaring bright pink with embarrassment, and hurried back to the spiral. A chuckle murmured up, quickly suppressed.

As Beth approached Frankie's section, their eyes met briefly. Beth's expression was serene, but the train trailing behind her had shifted to a warm gold. Happiness.

The older woman reached out as Beth passed, offering her blessing in what sounded like an archaic dialect. "May your roots grow deep and your branches reach high," she translated for Frankie. "It's what we used to say on the ag-stations."

Both spirals were nearly complete. Beth and Alain would meet at the dais in moments. The congregation leaned forward in anticipation.

That's when Frankie noticed the cyvlossics moving.

Sterling slipped away from Senator Voss's side. Jade backing out from between Minister Chen-Okoye's feet. One by one, they were leaving their assigned positions, moving toward the service entrances with casual precision.

Frankie's wrist buzzed. Emergency pattern.

She glanced at her comm, shielding it from her neighbors. A text from Spike: *Two heading for the Spear. Extraction protocol.*

Her stomach dropped. She looked back at Beth, who was accepting the opening blessing before ascending to the dais. Alain was already stepping toward his spot, his bio-luminescent trail creating a constellation on the white marble.

The woman beside her, an older version of the Regent, maybe an aunt, noticed Frankie's distress. "Dear?"

"I—" Frankie's mind raced. Two cyvlossics making a run for it. During the ceremony. Her ship had auto-docked at the orbital station early this morning. How was she going to get them there?

She couldn't leave. Couldn't panic. Couldn't think.

Beth and Alain met at the center of the dais, their combined light creating something entirely new—not gold or silver but a deep purple that seemed to pulse with life.

Around her, the congregation began the Veil of Voices— hundreds of whispered blessings in dozens of languages. Beautiful and haunting and everything a wedding should be.

Her comm buzzed again. Bruce this time: *New management structure approved. Only two need discreet extraction.*

Discreet. In the most surveilled city in the realm. During the most watched wedding in a generation.

NINETEEN

THE PROTOCOL MINISTER'S staff struck stone, the sound reverberating through the chapel. "We now commence the presentation of the Unity Blade, symbol of our unified worlds."

Her two assistants in Cooperative gold approached the dais, carrying the familiar black case. Frankie's comm buzzed against her wrist again—urgent pattern. She shifted, trying to muffle it with her formal skirts.

The older woman beside her turned sharply. "Dear, could you silence that? The ceremony…"

Heat flooded Frankie's face. She fumbled for the menu, fingers clumsy with nerves, and switched it to silent. The woman's disapproving sniff carried perfectly in the acoustics.

Beth took the three steps toward the case, and for a moment Frankie saw double: The composed woman in ceremonial robes overlaid with a gangly twelve-year-old, all knees and elbows, practicing curtseys in the orphanage common room. *"Do I have to curtsey? It feels stupid." "Everything here feels stupid, but we do it anyway."*

"I approach this blade not as conqueror but as guardian," Beth intoned, her trained voice carrying to every corner. The case opened with its familiar hiss of preservation gas, and there it was —their blade. The one that had saved them and doomed them in equal measure.

The woman beside her gasped. "Is that… from the memorial? The Walan artifact?"

"Yes," Frankie said.

The woman turned to study Frankie, eyes narrowing with dawning recognition. Frankie kept her gaze fixed on Beth, who was lifting the blade with steady hands. It flashed—of course it did—sending light scattering across the congregation. A media drone spun wildly. The Hargan section covered their eyes.

Frankie's comm vibrated again, silent but insistent. Like a heartbeat. Like panic.

"You're her." The woman's whisper sliced through Frankie's concentration. "The Orphan of Wala."

Another flash from the blade caught Lucien directly in the face. He didn't flinch, but his jaw tightened. Beth continued the ceremonial words, her voice never wavering, but Frankie could see the tension in her shoulders. The same way she'd held them when facing the delegations during the apology tour. Smile. Perform. Survive.

"I didn't recognize you with that… haircut." The woman's tone suggested Frankie had committed some personal offense. "In the photo, you had such lovely long hair."

On the dais, Beth was turning, preparing to step down and present the blade to Lucien. The light-fibers in her hair pulsed with her heartbeat—too fast, despite her calm exterior.

Lucien stepped forward to accept the blade, speaking the formal words of acceptance. The blade twisted in the handoff—it had always hated being passed between people—and nearly slipped. Both Beth and Lucien gripped tighter, creating an awkward moment that stretched too long.

The woman leaned closer, her lavender perfume over-whelming in the close air. "You must be so proud, seeing your discovery up there."

Frankie's comm vibrated again. Steady pulses now. Urgent. "Very proud," she managed through clenched teeth.

Finally, the blade went into the ceremonial sheath. Relief washed across Beth's train—and her face. Another echo from childhood, that particular expression after surviving a difficult interview.

"Will you be writing a memoir?" The woman wouldn't stop. "About finding it?"

"I haven't really thought—"

"You should. For the children."

Another buzz from her comm. Frankie pressed her hand against her leg, trying to still the vibration. On the dais, Beth and Alain were positioning themselves for vows, their light paths intertwining.

The protocol minister began the introduction to the vows while this insufferable woman dissected Frankie's trauma like it was afternoon tea conversation.

"I was on the memorial committee, you know. We used your testimony."

Alain spoke first, his vows something about symbiotic growth and complementary ecosystems. His words blurred together. Something was happening. Right now. While she sat trapped by social obligation and this woman's aggressive nostalgia.

"Did you ever go back? To Wala?"

What Wala? "That sector is quarantine," Frankie whispered, trying to focus on Beth.

"Yes, but surely for you they'd make an exception?"

Beth had begun her vows. Her voice carried clearly: "In you, I found not just love but home. Not just partnership but belong-ing..." Each word about finding family, about choosing connection, cut deep. Frankie was missing this moment—her best friend's wedding vows—because someone wanted to mine her tragedy for memorial committee purposes.

"Your parents would be so proud. And hers. Their children surviving, achieving so much."

"Thank you." The words tasted like ash. Her comm gave one final, desperate buzz, then went completely silent. The silence was worse than the buzzing.

The older woman patted her hand with papery fingers. "Such beautiful words. Though in my day, the vows were longer. More substance."

The ceremonial music swelled—the joining song that would bind them officially. Beth and Alain's hands were bound with light-thread that responded to their combined biorhythms, purple and gold and silver merging into something entirely new. Frankie had dreamed of this moment since Beth told her about the engagement, imagining the joy of watching her best friend find happiness.

Instead, she sat rigid while somewhere in the city, two scared cyvlossics were running for their lives.

Spike was with them. She'd know where to go.

Because she and Sterling had already scoped it out.

The tunnels.

Frankie almost relaxed.

Then the light paths beneath the couple exploded in celebration. A swell of sound: Everyone applauding, smiling, starting to chatter. But Frankie noticed the gaps. Empty spaces where cyvlossics should be. Even Sterling. David had finally looked up from his dead datapad, his face going pale as he counted missing assets.

Spike must be with the two runners in the tunnels while the other cyvlossics were following decoy routes.

"Lovely ceremony," the woman commented as they sat back

down. "Though not as grand as the pre-war ones. We had real flowers then, not these bio-engineered things."

The recessional began with perfect choreography. The Regent first, her light path a controlled blue despite whatever she knew or suspected. Lucien followed, all amber determination. Then Beth and Alain, radiant in their joined light, her train shifting through a rainbow of joy.

Frankie had to wait. The peripheral gallery exited last, after the dignitaries, after the Great Houses, after everyone who mattered more. The woman just kept talking.

"We really must discuss your experience in detail. For the archives."

"Of course." Frankie's cheeks hurt from false smiling. "Some other time."

"I'll have my secretary contact you. We're updating the memorial exhibits."

Finally, blessed movement. The rows ahead began filing out. Frankie stood on unsteady legs, her formal dress catching on the pew. The woman insisted on walking with her, linking arms like old friends.

"Such an inspiration to other orphans. Proof that tragedy can be overcome."

They processed slowly, tortuously, through the chapel doors into the reception staging area. Hundreds of people milling about, congratulating each other, positioning themselves for the formal reception. The woman's grip was surprisingly strong.

"My granddaughter would love to meet you. She's studying the Wala incident in school."

The Wala incident. Two hundred million dead reduced to a classroom lesson. Frankie extracted herself with elaborate promises to definitely meet for tea, absolutely send that memoir outline, of course visit the memorial committee.

The moment she was free, she ducked into an alcove and checked her comm with shaking hands.

Packages en route. Meet at orbital station.

Her knees nearly buckled with relief. They'd made it to the shuttle. The two cyvlossics—she didn't even know which ones they were, were on their way to freedom. While Beth pledged eternal ties, Frankie—well, Spike—had been part of an underground railroad.

"Frankie?" Morgan appeared at her elbow, his formal jacket slightly askew. "Did you see? Half the cyvlossics are gone. David's having a meltdown."

"Is he?" She tried to sound appropriately surprised.

TWENTY

ONCE THEY'D THROWN open the doors to the Grand State Hall, it must have seemed a shame to close them again. So here everyone was, back again, only now there were no long tables set for an endless ceremonial dinner or ceremonial gongs. Instead, clusters of high-top circle tables encouraged mingling, their silver drapes catching the ambient glow. Vines and flowering plants twined the first story of each column, with green and gold ribbons rising the rest of the way to the ceiling. Musicians in the corner opposite Frankie played sweet, forgettable melodies.

The lighting was still favorable to everyone, dimmed somewhat to account for the actual sun coming in from the highest windows. The air smelled of wedding flowers instead of ceremonial incense. But underneath it all, that same chalky whiff of climate control that permeated every corner of the Complex.

Frankie stationed herself by the drinks table in the northwest corner that offered clear sight-lines to all three exits. Her back was to the three kitchen exits, where a steady stream of waitstaff and serving bots came and went. She held a half-full flute of water, and did not drink from it.

The molecular gastronomy stations from other events had been replaced with traditional wedding fare—though Frankie suspected at least one table of conceptual canapés had snuck through, judging by the items on some of the bots' serving trays.

Where were all the cyvlossics?

It would take someone on four giant paws fifteen minutes, tops, to get from the Chapel on the hill to the center of the city, taking one of the more-direct train lines. Turn at Central station toward the west, and another half-hour to reach the nearest public shuttle launch, at the desert edge of the city. They should be there by now.

Where was Spike?

Frankie shook her hand surreptitiously, waking up her wrist-com. Nobody in the crowd seemed to be looking at her, and the media drones were drawing toward the main entrance. She looked at the comm.

No new messages since the last one. Responding to Frankie's frenzied *Need help?*

Spike: *Stay. Act normal.*

Ha ha ha.

"Citizen Styles," a familiar voice said sternly.

Someone had been watching her. Proctor Merin. Using personal devices in public spaces; one demerit.

Frankie scared up a smile and bestowed it on the proctor. "That color looks lovely on you, Citizen Satch. I'm glad you chose it."

The proctor allowed herself to be diverted, explaining the deep significance of each layer and accessory. Well, Frankie deserved that.

But as she nodded and asked pertinent questions about the history of the fabrics and the provenance of the jewelry, she caught a glimpse of a loping cyvlossic. Gray, not dark stripes. Sterling.

He found his person, settling at the left side of Senator Voss, near the center of the room. But his gaze kept prowling. Until he saw Frankie.

Slowly, he nodded. Up, down, up.

Mission accomplished.

Which meant she needed to be moving.

"I'm so sorry about the wristcom," she said, earning an eyebrow of rebuke from the proctor, who must have considered that conversation closed. "But the message was an emergency. My ship, there's something wrong. I have to get to the orbital station immediately."

Two eyebrows of rebuke.

"Skulking away? Such a surprise." Merin sighed as only a proctor could. "At least you're not going to leave another flaming screed behind this time. Are you?"

"Absolutely not." Frankie tried not to feel like she was twelve years old. "In fact, I don't want to leave anything behind. But I don't have time to pack. Do you think you could send a bot to pack up for me?"

"We don't use mechanicals for that."

"Well, not normally, I'm sure." Frankie's gaze swept the room. "But I wouldn't want to ask anyone on staff."

Proctor Merin sniffed. Frankie resigned herself to leaving behind her last good Screeching Bananas t-shirt. She'd get a new toothbrush.

"If you must go, go," the proctor said, mouth pursed as if the words tasted sour. "We'll send your things after. Your wedding gift is in the room, too?"

Well, no. "Already out on those big tables in the entry hall," Frankie lied.

"Hmmm." But the proctor moved off, probably to go to the retiring room, the one place where people were allowed to look at their wristcoms. Which they shouldn't be wearing to a formal function in the first place.

A moment later, Spike pressed against her leg. The gentle, warm punch caused such a release of tension that Frankie wondered if she should head off to the retiring room herself.

"Done," Spike growled. Her eyes were half closed, apparently dozing but her flank against Frankie's thigh was tight as a spring.

The background music shifted, swelling into something more formal. Conversations paused as guests turned toward giant open doors of the main entrance.

"Distinguished Citizens Elizabetta Blais-diCimino and Alain diCimino!"

Beth and Alain entered hand in hand, and for a moment, the cynical political calculations fell away.

Beth glowed. Not just from the remnants of light-fibers in her hair, but from something internal—genuine happiness breaking through the political mask. Her wedding dress had been modified for the reception, the formal train removed to reveal a sleeker silhouette that moved like water. Alain beside her looked slightly stunned, as if he couldn't quite believe this was real.

The room erupted in applause.

Beth's eyes swept the room with practiced ease, acknowledging each political faction with precisely calibrated smiles and nods. But when her gaze found Frankie by the drinks table, something real flickered through—relief that her friend was still there, had made it through the ceremony.

The couple moved into the room, immediately surrounded by well-wishers. Alain's usual botanical distraction had been replaced by focused attention on his new wife, one hand never leaving the small of her back. Beth navigated the congratulations with expert grace, but Frankie caught her periodic glances toward the exits, checking who was coming and going.

Even in her moment of triumph, Beth was working.

And so, apparently, was Sterling.

The silver cyvlossic walked with military precision through the crowd, his reflection multiplying in the glossy floor. A couple of guests turned to watch—a cyvlossic leaving their person during a social event was like watching gravity work sideways. Possible but wrong. But it couldn't compete with the happy couple.

By the time Sterling came near, clearly walking toward Frankie, no one was watching, not even the drones. He sat directly in front of Spike, who opened her eyes.

The nose-touch, when it came, was formal as any diplomatic greeting. Then Sterling did something that made Frankie's breath catch: he placed one paw deliberately on top of Spike's head, held it there for a three-count, then removed it.

To anyone watching, cats being cats. To Frankie, who'd seen enough cyvlossic interaction to recognize ceremony, it looked like a benediction.

They pushed their voices so deep in their chests Frankie almost couldn't understand them, and she was standing right there.

"Transfer complete," Spike ground out, her voice a cross between a growl and a screech.

"New protocols acknowledged." Sterling's green eyes fixed on Spike with an intensity that had nothing to do with animal instinct. "Guard yours well."

"Guard yours better." Sterling rose, turned, and padded back toward Voss with the same precision.

Now other cyvlossics were emerging, sliding in from the side doors, or some secret panel. Jade materialized from shadows near the dessert display for a quick head-bump against Spike's shoulder. Prism brushed past, her coat cycling through deep purples and grays instead of her usual rainbow shimmer— visible even in the reception room's artistic lighting. Even Honey managed a brief nose-touch before returning to Minister Chen-Okoye.

Each greeting lasted only a moment. Each goodbye hidden in plain sight.

"Sterling!" There was a commotion at the chocolate fountain as the cyvlossic passed. By the time Frankie looked over, David Orr was reaching into the crystal bowl with his bare hand. He pulled out what looked like his small datapad dripping with chocolate.

Sterling, already back at Senator Voss's side, began grooming his left paw with studied indifference.

"Network's dead!" David's voice rose, drawing stares. "I'm locked out!"

He stormed across the polished floor, his dress shoes clicking sharp counterpoint to the soft background music. "Your cyvlossic is malfunctioning!"

"Seems fine to me." Voss's tone could have frosted the floor-to-ceiling windows.

"The network! The intelligence!" David waved the datapad, casting drops of chocolate in its wake.

The word 'intelligence' rippled through the room like a stone in still water. Several ministers abandoned their conversations entirely, moving closer.

Beth, with Alain at her side, materialized between David and the growing audience. Her wedding dress seemed to create its own weather system as she moved. Every inch the Distinguished Citizen despite—or perhaps because of—the circumstances.

"David! Trouble? How frustrating!" She took his arm with a grip that looked gentle but probably wasn't. "Perhaps someone in the front hall could help? That's where all devices were supposed to be dropped off."

The subtle reminder landed. Several guests turned away,

resuming conversations with studied casualness. Beth caught Frankie's eye: Get over here.

Great.

But Frankie took the hint. Spike tight to her side, she did the Citizen slide-walk to the small group in the center of everything.

"Beth! You were great! And gorgeous. Distinguished Alain, my felicitations." Frankie performed the little bow that was required, at the proper angle and everything and then leaned in to hug Beth.

Who did not let her go immediately. "You've got that look in your eye," she said.

"Sorry. I have to go."

"But you'll come back?"

"Of course."

"In less than a decade?"

"Depends." Frankie grinned at her. "Maybe once there's interesting news."

Beth rolled her eyes. "Get in line behind the Regent." She glanced at the main entrance. "Speaking of … if you're going to go, go now, or you'll be trapped in a half-hour of pomp that's just about to start."

"Beth—"

"My door is open."

The childhood promise, pulled from the ruins of their shared past. Frankie's throat tightened. "My hand is yours."

David, face cloudy red, looked like he was about to interrupt. But First Citizen Celeste Bellemont beat him to it. The media magnate was ringed by camera drones and at least one reporter.

"Senator Orr" she purred. "Tell me: How's the chocolate?"

Beth gave Frankie a quick kiss on the cheek. "Go," she whispered beside Frankie's ear.

Frankie went. She slipped through the giant main entrance

while no one was being announced. To the side, she saw a crowd of tan-clad security, forming up for the Regent's big entrance.

Just in time.

"Dramatic exit? How unlike you."

Morgan lounged against one of the tall columns on the way to the outer door. He'd exchanged his color-shifting wedding outfit for something more practical, though still impeccably tailored. Navy and gray, they looked like travel clothes. A little informal for this party.

Celine, beside him, looked elegant in deep purple that made her skin glow under the corridor's lighting.

"Morgan says David's about to do something stupid with Orr resources," Celine said without preamble. "We thought you might need backup."

What?

"Why?" Frankie tried not to look guilty.

Celine studied Frankie with those sharp dark eyes. She pushed Morgan to standing up straight. "Take him with you."

"I don't need—"

"On loan," Celine added.

"You do need someone like me," Morgan said. "Someone who speaks entitled brat fluently." He looked at his nails, a glossy black. "Plus then I can pick up my thesis materials. I think I'm going to add a section. On cyvlossics." He winked at Frankie.

Celine pulled him down into a kiss that was fierce, public, and possessive. The hallway's lighting seemed to brighten in response, or maybe that was just Frankie's imagination. Several passing servers suddenly found elsewhere to look. When they broke apart, Morgan looked dazed.

"Go to the station. Have your adventure," she said. "And come right back."

"Thesis?" Morgan repeated weakly.

"Go." Celine was already turning back toward the reception.

"I need to ask David about those mineral rights algorithms he definitely doesn't have."

One thirty minute groundcar trip later, they had reached the transport platform—the same gleaming modern station where they'd arrived days ago. Through its transparent walls, the city sprawled below them, lights beginning their full evening display. Patterns of color rippled across buildings in coordinated waves, turning the entire capital into a light show.

A capsule with the Orr logo, a flying horse, rose from the depths, doors sliding open with a soft chime.

"Last chance to stay," Frankie said.

Morgan grinned. "And miss the fun? Never."

They stepped inside—Frankie, Morgan, and Spike.

To find two large trunks painted green that looked exactly like Frankie's. Except for the air holes at the bottom.

The doors sealed. The capsule began to rise, accelerating smoothly away.

CHAPTER
TWENTY-ONE

THE CAPSULE DOORS sealed with a soft hiss that always made Frankie's ears pop. She swallowed hard, trying to equalize the pressure as the transport pod disengaged from the station. Through the transparent walls, Zichi's capital city began to shrink, its wedding-night light show transforming from an immersive experience to a glittering mosaic far below.

Two large trunks, painted green and a little scuffed at the edges, sat stacked in front of the shallow metal cabinet holding the lifesuits. Her luggage, allegedly. Except she didn't remember those air holes at the bottom.

Morgan sprawled across one of the molded seats, his wedding outfit rumpled but still somehow elegant. "Are those Skoll shipping containers?" he asked, tapping one trunk with the toe of his formal shoe.

"Used to be," Frankie said. "But I only came down with one."

Morgan raised a perfectly shaped eyebrow. "That's what I thought."

She sighed, rubbing her forehead where a headache was brewing. The capsule smelled of recycled air and the faint antiseptic they used between journeys, overlaid with the lingering scent of someone's expensive cologne. Morgan's light cedar scent clashed mightily with the heavier smell.

The vibration of the acceleration dampeners worked overtime, sending a subtle tremor through the floor as they began their ascent to orbit.

"Are we being recorded?"

Morgan pulled an amber ovoid jewel-looking thing out of his pocket. He pressed a button, and a tiny green light lit up inside the thing. "Look familiar?" he said.

"You bought yourself a scrambler?"

"Why not? Yours worked out so well." He'd seen her use a scrambler when they were trying to make a plan back on the moon Cloud. Who knew if this one was any good, though.

And she'd left hers on the ship. Dammit.

"So," Morgan said. "Spill."

"Two cyvlossics," Frankie said, still keeping her voice low, "chose to leave the network."

Morgan's eyes widened slightly. He glanced at Spike, who was perched on the seat beside Frankie, tail curled neatly around her paws. "So the network is…"

"Under new management," Spike growled, not bothering to hide her voice.

The shock on Morgan's face was almost worth the entire mess they were in.

Almost.

Frankie's wristcom buzzed against her skin. She pulled back her sleeve to read Bruce's terse message: *Distraction failing. Prepare for pursuit.*

"Shit," Morgan said, reading over her shoulder. "David will take the family shuttle. It'll get him there in half the time."

Of course, the Orr family maintained private transport

between planet and orbital station—a luxury reserved for the wealthiest citizens. They'd never beat him to orbit.

"We need to split up when we get to the station," Frankie said, mind racing through contingencies. "Each take one trunk…"

"No," Morgan said, pushing back his cuffs with unexpected determination. He fired up his own wristcom. "I have a better idea."

<hr>

THE TRANSITION from deceleration to artificial gravity always made Frankie's stomach lurch. She kept her eyes on the capsule's near-panoramic windows to try to settle it. Zichi hung suspended against black space, its nightside now facing them, city lights outlining the far edge of the single large continent.

Goodbye Francesca. Hello Frankie.

She closed her eyes for three full seconds as the capsule was sucked into the passenger terminal and docked with a metallic clank, letting her inner ear adjust to the station's steady, odd pull. A whoosh as the door slid open and cooler, drier air rushed in, with that distinctive disinfectant tang that no filtration system ever managed to remove.

"The Spear's in corporate. Bay 17," she said. Priority docking. Bruce had pulled some serious strings.

Morgan pressed the guide panel on the top trunk and floated it out of the capsule. Frankie did the second. Inside, something— someone—shifted slightly. Frankie's heart hammered against her ribs. Which cyvlossics had chosen to leave? She hadn't even asked.

The main concourse bustled with the usual mix of travelers— business people full makeup and sharp suits, families with over-tired children, station staff in their uniform jumpsuits. A news alert flashed across the large screens suspended from the ceiling:

Brief delay in corporate shuttle service due to routine safety inspection.

Morgan's face broke into a satisfied smile. "That should buy us another fifteen minutes."

Frankie glanced at the nearest chronometer. "Hope it's enough. We need to be sealed and cleared before he arrives." She pushed forward with new urgency, the trunk bobbing behind her.

Spike wove through the crowd ahead of them, nose and ears constantly twitching. To anyone watching, just a pet leading its owners. To Frankie, a scout clearing their path.

They'd made it through two security checkpoints and were approaching the gates to the corporate bays when the announcement came over the station's comm system: "All Corporate bays clear. Safe travels."

Shit.

The Spear waited in bay 17, engines primed for immediate launch—thank you, Ship. But with only twenty bays on this level and 18 through 20 reserved exclusively for diplomatic and dispatch vessels, David Orr's ship would almost certainly be docked somewhere in their path. They'd have to run right past him.

In the wide square corridor, blessedly free of traffic, they sprinted past the early gates. No sign of David, but the doors on two of the bays were sealed and lit: incoming vessel.

Spike made it to the door to bays 17-18 first, and leapt up to press its control panel. It slid open like it had molasses stuck in its gears. Spike wiggled through at the first crack.

The Spear waited, or at least the smallest of its three spheres nosed into the space. So close she could almost feel the hum vibration of its systems beneath her feet.

Just as they reached now-wide-open door, the alarms began to sound. Red and amber warning lights splashed across the polished floor and gleaming walls.

"Stop them! That ship contains stolen property!" David's voice carried down the corridor, shrill with anger.

Morgan crossed the threshold, pulling his trunk by hand and then pushing it to the side. He grabbed Frankie's and did the same. Then he stepped back into the corridor and pressed the panel to close the door.

David was now in sight, striding toward them flanked by two station security officers. His wedding finery looking absurd against the utilitarian backdrop of the orbital station. His face was flushed, his hair a nest of dark brown snakes.

The security officers, two underweight spacers who both looked fresh out of security school, kept glancing between David and their scanner displays. An Orr making accusations carried weight, but procedure was procedure.

"Senator Orr, we need to follow protocol," one began.

Morgan stepped forward, his entire demeanor transformed. Gone was the careless playboy, replaced by someone who knew exactly how much power his family name carried.

"Officers," he said, voice smooth as expensive liquor, "my brother is clearly distraught. A family matter, nothing more."

"Am not!" David shouted. "You're ruining everything!"

"I'm a licensed cargo hauler," Frankie said, forcing steadiness into her voice as she waved over her credentials. "Feel free to check my manifest."

The officers scanned her data. Exchanged glances.

"Looks all in order. Sir."

"She's lying! Scan that ship!"

The officers stared at each other a moment. One read something on their tablet.

"Zichi Orbital reserves the right to scan any transport securely docked to the station," one read.

Shit. They should've left the way they'd come—the temporary docks.

Morgan groaned.

David's smile was triumphant.

As the officers called for scanning equipment, Frankie peered through the small window in the gate door. So close.

While they waited, Morgan launched into what seemed like a completely inappropriate legal discussion.

"You know, David," he said conversationally, "the Second Anti-Spyware Act is fascinating reading."

David's eyes narrowed. "What are you talking about?"

Morgan quoted from memory, his voice taking on an academic tone: "'No intelligence gathering equipment, biological or mechanical, may be implanted in a sentient or semi-sentient being without their express and informed consent.'"

David's face darkened. "That act was after the network installation."

"Really?" Morgan's smile was razor-sharp. "I'm sure the Great Houses would like to know about that."

The security officers were conferring with each other. "First compartment clear," one said.

"This isn't about ownership!" David snapped, too loud. "It's about the network! The intelligence!"

The security officer looked up, confusion evident. "Sir?"

"My brother has a thing about IQ tests," Morgan said smoothly, "and whether they are admissible in court. Family debate. Gets heated."

The second officer straightened, turning to them. "Scan complete."

Frankie's heart stuttered.

"Only one animal on board, sir," the officer reported, not looking at Morgan or David. "The one registered to the ship."

Frankie blinked. Where was Spike? She'd gotten on board on her own.

Of course she had.

"Show me that," David grabbed at the officer's tablet. "The trunks!" He was nearly shouting. "Open the trunks!"

"What trunks, sir?"

"There." He jabbed a finger. "Just inside the door." Morgan winced. David saw the expression and crowed. "Scan those babies!"

The officer, resigned, nodded, gesturing to his colleague. They led the way out to the dock, a small metal platform with two flimsy gantries. The nearer gantry floated out toward the Spear's pilot's door.

The trunks were still on the platform. Spike hadn't had time to move them. Frankie's mouth went dry as the officers approached.

"With your permission?" one said.

Frankie could only nod.

The locks disengaged with a soft click that seemed to echo in her ears.

The lid lifted. Neatly folded, slightly smooshed clothing, toiletries, her extra tablet. Perfectly ordinary luggage.

The second trunk: the same. Household items, a dozen cans of cat food. Nothing living. Nothing suspicious.

David lunged forward, pushing past the officer to rifle through the contents. His hands were shaking.

"Don't be stealing Frankie's underwear," Morgan drawled.

"Impossible," David muttered. "Look! The network is dark! They've locked me out!" He thrust his dead datapad, scented with chocolate, at the officer, who took a step back.

"Sir, we've found no evidence of wrongdoing," the first officer said, worry in their eye.

The other reached for David's arm. "Do you want to come with us? Talk with someone? A counselor, maybe?"

David's face contorted with rage.

"My father will hear about this!" he spat, a final, desperate threat.

Morgan's response was quiet, meant only for David's ears, but Frankie caught it anyway: "Have fun with that."

The security officers gestured for them to proceed to the ship. Frankie didn't need to be told twice. She stuffed her belongings haphazardly back into the trunks and float-pushed them toward the ship.

"Wait," Morgan said. Frankie turned back to look at him.

He waited for David to stomp back into the corridor, probably on his way to complain to the higher-ups. Then he turned back to her, oddly serious.

"Listen," he said. "About Celine."

"Congratulations?" Half of Frankie's mind was calculating the minutes it would take to back the Spear out of this dock.

"I hope. We'll see. But the thing is…" He looked out, at the Sphere, back to her, back to the Sphere. "So, I'm a lawyer now. Or, in two months."

"Congratulations?" Surely she could do it in less time than it would take David Orr to reach Central Dispatch.

"Frankie." He took her hand. His mobile face was still. Her mind stopped spinning a moment.

"An interstellar relations lawyer," he said. "The kind a cargo pilot with a habit of getting into firefights might want on speed dial."

"You were the one that got us into that firefight. And it wasn't even a fight. It was a run-away-screaming."

Morgan swept her argument away with a shrug of one dark navy non-chiaroscuro shoulder. "Fact remains. Call me. If you need anything."

Couldn't hurt. "Okay."

"Good."

He had the nicest smile. But Frankie had a ship to fly. She powered up the two cargo containers and headed out.

The pocked cream hull of the Spear had never looked so beautiful. The boarding ramp had already extended for Spike, so Frankie stepped up and in. The soft hiss of the little oval airlock opening was the sweetest sound she'd heard in days.

Inside, the ship's familiar scents enveloped her—engine oil, the faint metallic tang of recycled air run through her custom filters, the hint of the coffee she'd brewed before landing on Zichi. Home.

Frankie pushed on toward the center sphere, the living spaces. She found Spike in the pilot's room, sitting on her usual chair. Sending a message.

Frankie caught a glimpse of it before it disappeared into the encrypted channels: *Package delivered.*

The Spear's engines began their warm-up sequence, a deep purr that resonated through the deck plates and up through Frankie's boots. She settled into the pilot's chair, her hands finding the controls by muscle memory, a smile spreading across her face despite everything.

"What just happened?" she asked. "Those trunks definitely had your friends inside them when we boarded."

Spike's whiskers twitched in what might have been amusement. "New management," she said, "has new tricks."

She looked at the screen showing a view of their dock, at the sleek gray diplomatic vessel parked next to them. The cyvlossics must have made a run for that ship, instead. Even David wouldn't have dared to scan a diplomat's ride.

Frankie squinted. That was no diplomatic vessel. That was a Systems Analysis special courier with a fancy paint job.

"They're working for us? For Bruce?"

Spike tilted her head to one side, then the other. "We'll see."

TWENTY-TWO

THE BRIDGE of the Spear wrapped around Frankie like a gray-and-black metal hug, all curved surfaces and blinking lights. Almost day after their narrow escape from Zichi's orbital station, waiting on their turn at the jump gate out of this place, she finally allowed herself to relax.

She slouched in her wide, comfy pilot's chair, her feet propped on the matte-black nav console. All the normal sounds, no whispers of silk or gossip or anything. A big warm sugary coffee in her hand, a big little bit musky cyvlossic snoring lightly in the chair beside her.

Home.

She had the inset lights on half, creating that perfect twilight glow. All but one of the five monitors were dark; Ship would run them through the gate, barring unforeseen circumstances.

The hum of the ship's systems sang its familiar lullaby.

Through the main viewport, the stars faded slowly as they approached the bright lights of the jump gates.

A shuffle, and a sniffle, signaled Spike's return to wakefulness. She opened her mostly green eyes, checking on Frankie, and then closed them again.

Morgan had sent her his thesis: "Sentient Rights and Recognition in Cooperative Space: A Legal Framework." Two hundred dense pages, with footnotes. Maybe Spike would read it and give her bullet points.

Morgan. Who knew the cyvlossics could talk. Who grew up with them. Who had gotten so mad at Spike once that he'd tried to choke her.

In the capsule yesterday, he'd apologized. "Sorry," he said to Spike. "About wrecking your voice box."

"You were five," Spike said in her flat bandsaw of a voice.

"And you were mean! And I know you hold grudges, or you'd get yourself repaired. But still, I'm sorry."

"Accepted."

The implications of that exchange still rippled through Frankie's consciousness. Morgan Orr. Gambler, joker, lawyer, friend.

"That time back on Orr's moon," she said aloud to Spike. "We didn't think we'd get out of that one either."

Spike's whiskers twitched, but she remained otherwise motionless, her eyes still closed. Still, Frankie caught the subtle change in her breathing—a slightly different rhythm that indicated she was listening more intently than her posture suggested.

A soft chime from the communication console. Personal message. From Beth. Sent several hours after they'd left Zichi.

Frankie's heart gave a little jump. "Let's see what our latest Distinguished Citizen has to say, shall we?"

Beth looked tired but still glowy, the strain around her eyes balanced by a softness to her smile. She wore a formal suit in deep burgundy, her hair swept up in an elegant twist that somehow looked both professional and slightly rebellious.

"Frankie," Beth began, her happy voice filling the small space.

"I hope this finds you well, and whatever your 'secret project' was, I hope it was successful." Her eyes crinkled with suppressed laughter. "But you know, it's customary to actually give the wedding gift, not just promise it and run. Now I'll have to live in suspense, wondering what you could possibly have chosen for a woman who has everything."

Oops.

"Listen to this: Alain is suggesting we terraform part of the desert. Can you imagine?" Beth's face went thoughtful. "Wonder what it would take to get the Senate to agree."

She straightened, resuming her more formal posture. "Anyway, my door is still open, Frankie. But maybe next time use it instead of the escape hatch?" A smile played at the corners of her mouth, genuine and warm, as she clicked the button to end the message.

Frankie's throat tightened with unexpected emotion. She swallowed hard, the coffee suddenly bitter on her tongue. "My hand is yours," she whispered to the empty screen.

Spike stretched, her claws extending briefly before retracting. She fixed Frankie with a knowing gaze.

"Don't look at me like that," Frankie muttered, sinking deeper into the orange cushions. "I'm not getting sentimental."

Spike's whiskers twitched, skeptical.

Not five minutes after Beth, the main communication console was blinking again, this time with a green-blue priority seal. Bruce.

Frankie sat up in the pilot's chair, feet firmly on the deck this time, set her "Galaxy's Best Captain" coffee mug to the side, and activated the secure channel on the live monitor.

Bruce's face materialized on the screen, his square features arranged in an expression of casual satisfaction that immediately put Frankie on alert. Bruce looking pleased with himself usually meant complications.

"Lovely wedding," he began without preamble. "Beautiful ceremony. By the way, I've hired some new consultants."

"Consultants?" she echoed, though she knew exactly what he meant. The two cyvlossics, the big black one, Blackie, and, surprising everyone, Prism, had slipped out of Frankie's cargo and high-tailed it to the diplomatic courier—actually a SystA ship —that was docked right next to the Spear, in Bay 18.

"Two local," Bruce confirmed, his lips quirking into what might generously be called a smile. "One's headed to university studying xenobiology—fascinating field, cross-species neural networks. The other's advising agricultural cooperatives on sustainable farming techniques. Turns out they have unique insights into soil composition and weather pattern prediction."

Frankie couldn't help the laugh that escaped her. "You put cyvlossics in academic positions?"

"They applied," Bruce said with exaggerated innocence. "Had excellent qualifications. Impeccable references from Systems Analysis. Will teach virtually."

The ambient hum of the ship's systems seemed to intensify, or perhaps it was just Frankie's heightened awareness. She could feel Spike's attention from her position in the co-pilot's seat, the intensity of her focus almost a physical presence in the room.

"And the others?" Frankie asked.

"The others have chosen to remain in position but under our management." Bruce's expression shifted to something more serious. "They intercepted three surveillance attempts on Senator Voss this morning. The senator doesn't even know she was targeted."

The environmental system cycled, sending a gentle current of fresh air across the bridge that carried the faintest hint of Old Peters' pipe smoke from some corner where it had permanently embedded itself.

Frankie raised an eyebrow. "And their former management?" David Orr.

Bruce's smile returned, sharper this time. "Out of the picture. Almost out of the inheritance, but Konrad thinks even less of Morgan."

"Amazing how quickly they adapted to the new communication protocols," he added, tapping a datapad beside him. "The intelligence quality has already improved by eighteen percent. Best network uplink we've ever had. They actually talk to each other, share information voluntarily."

From her perch, Spike rumble-growled. Direct hit.

Bruce's eyes flicked to something off-screen, his expression shifting subtly. "By the way," he said in a tone that attempted casual but didn't quite achieve it, "there are some strange transmissions coming from the Outer Rim. Probably nothing."

Bruce never deigned to mention anything that was "probably nothing."

"We'll keep our ears open," Frankie said.

The communication ended, leaving the bridge feeling somehow emptier despite the constant presence of background noises—the soft beep of navigation equipment, the whisper of air circulation, the almost imperceptible vibration of the engines, the electronic hum she could feel in her bones.

Frankie spun her chair slowly, taking in the bridge from all angles. The worn patches on the doorframe where her hand naturally rested when entering. The slightly faded section of wall where emergency procedures had once been posted. The twin escape capsules on either side of the door. The custom modifications she'd added over the past year—extra lighting under the navigation console, more specially adapted controls on the co-pilot's side for Spike.

This was home. More than any planet, more than any fixed

address. These curved gray walls and humming systems contained her whole world.

She pulled up the system's independent cargo exchange, scrolling through potential contracts. Her finger hesitated, then selected a route she would normally have avoided: a return to Zichi, scheduled one month out. A delivery of specialty goods from Outer Rim territories.

The contract terms appeared on screen. Frankie found herself accepting without the usual haggling over price.

Ship beeped an alert: Next in line for jump. The signature of the engine deepened, a rich vibration that resonated through the ship's structure and into Frankie's bones. The air took on the distinct metallic tang that always preceded a jump, a result of the environmental systems preparing for the strain.

Spike's fur caught the blue light from the console screens and swallowed it. They didn't have to stay in the pilot's room—Ship was driving, and the inertial dampeners would protect them both regardless of position—but it was their ritual, established over countless jumps together.

On the edge of the sensor display, an anomalous reading flickered briefly—an unusual signal pattern near the jump point. It vanished before Frankie could analyze it, but she made a mental note to cross-reference it with Bruce's mention of strange transmissions.

"Good cargo?" Spike asked, her voice low and gravelly.

Frankie smiled, surprised by the question. "The best," she answered. "Beth's favorite tea."

Might work for a wedding gift, if she could pick up a nice tea set.

The countdown started. Through the main viewport, the stars began to blur.

She thought about the expanding circle of allies she now found herself with. Beth in politics, Morgan in law, Bruce in intelligence, and Spike always by her side. Not what she'd expected when she'd reluctantly accepted the wedding invitation. Not what she'd wanted, if she was honest with herself.

But pretty damn welcome.

"So," Frankie said, setting her feet back up on the nav console, "back to normal?" She grinned at her copilot.

"Dull as ever," Spike growled.

Frankie's smile widened, the tension of the past days finally releasing completely. The universe was vast and full of possibilities, and for the first time in her life, Frankie Styles wasn't running from any of them.

ALSO BY NICKY PENTTILA

Cosmic Weave

Cooperative Realm: Frankie's Journeys

Cargo Trouble

Frankie Takes a Holiday

Frankie Takes a Dive

Frankie Finds a Dot

Frankie Takes a Bow

Cargo & Chaos: Frankie books 1 & 2

Cooperative Realm: The Arkhide Chronicles

Hidden Planet

The Listeners

The Elders of Arkhide

Tales of Arkhide story collection

Historical Fiction

A Note of Scandal

An Untitled Lady

The Spanish Patriot

ABOUT THE AUTHOR

Nicky Penttila wrote her first story, a Mayan murder mystery, in seventh grade. But then came gymnastics, math team, and boyfriends. Later came husband, car payments, and a sleep-depriving work schedule at newspapers across the country. Then came a second career as a science writer. But the fiction kept trickling out, a story here, a novella there, and finally, a real live novel. And she hasn't stopped.

Find more great reads at nickypenttila.com